Tw[illegible]
mur[illegible]
Burea[illegible] Drugs,
was ou[illegible]heir deaths.
The ma[illegible] for was Jacques
Brizard, [illegible]nable spider at the
centre of [illegible] world's biggest narcotic
operations and surrounded by an
apparently impenetrable wall of thugs and
political influence.

Ventura was desperate and the law was powerless to help. There was only one man who had the know-how and guts to do the job properly and that was Johnny Deray—the most expensive professional assassin in the business . . .

The Marseilles Contract

William Hughes

CORGI BOOKS
A DIVISION OF TRANSWORLD PUBLISHERS LTD

THE MARSEILLES CONTRACT
A CORGI BOOK 0 552 09687 3

First publication in Great Britain 1974

PRINTING HISTORY
Corgi edition published 1974

Corgi Books are published by
Transworld Publishers Ltd.,
Cavendish House,
57-59 Uxbridge Road,
Ealing, London, W.5

Made and printed in the United States of America
by Arcata Graphics
Buffalo, New York

TO EWA
FOR PATIENT UNDERSTANDING

The Marseilles Contract

CHAPTER ONE

The only warning of impending death came to Frank Matthews from that instinct for self-preservation which obeys the natural laws and is buried deep in every man. Now, as he walked to the steps at the end of the rain-swept cul-de-sac, it caused him to turn as the driver of the Citroen gunned the machine forward. The car's V-shaped snout seemed to dip to him just before it crushed his legs and pelvis, pinning him against the railings. All he gained from the last minute turn was a chance to see the men who were killing him.

After the initial impact, he felt no particular pain. Held upright by the weight of the car, he found that he was rapidly immersed in a thickening blanket of warmth. He watched the activity which now took place almost as if he was a disinterested observer. Calmet, the man who was sitting in the front passenger seat, was the only man to move. The rain glistened on the thick lenses of his spectacles as he paced briskly forward, the water settled on his close-cropped grey hair. No one who knew Calmet had ever seen him display any emotion and the sight of Matthews dying before his eyes produced none now, though the American had come as close as any man to endangering the organisation which Calmet served. His face retained the wooden look that sent a shiver of fear down the men against whom it was directed.

He stood by the bonnet, leant forward and opened the dying man's coat and jacket, to remove the precious package of white powder that had been the bait to the trap in this game of death. The drug was the real thing, almost a thousand dollars worth; Calmet was too much of an artist to use substitutes in his work. He slipped it into the pocket of the tightly-buttoned overcoat, turned away sharply and climbed back into the car, slamming the door.

Matthews was numb; wrapped in the warm blanket that killed all pain, the blanket of an approaching death: unaware that his life was ebbing away, watching the steady beat of the car's windscreen wipers, and, through the wet glass, the blurred faces of the four men who worked for Jacques Brizard.

There was Kurt, tall, lean, with darting eyes that missed nothing. He was the driver; Calmet sat next to him, principal lieutenant and organiser for Jacques Brizard, the man who helped him keep the crime of Marseilles under his control. In the back sat Wilson and Fortuit, two of Calmet's thugs.

There was a moment of stillness for Matthews, as if time had been suspended and he would remain caught between the car and the railings forever; then, with a roar, the car backed off him and he felt a sudden renewal of pain as the blanket was whipped away from him and his unsupported body fell forward on to the wet cobblestones shining in the weak street lighting of the old Paris Street.

The pain lasted only for a fleeting instant, then the blanket was back, enveloping him within its folds, welcoming him. He seemed to see his wife Rita and his young son Kevin standing a little distance off, watching him and waving to him. He wanted to smile, call out, reach up to them, but no sound came and the effort of movement seemed too much, so he just lay within his warm cocoon, watching them with love in his heart, feeling nothing from the waist down, the only sensation being the dampness of the rain on his face.

Beyond his now limited and receding line of vision, the car had come to an abrupt halt outside the only lighted window in the short street—the frontage of a small cafe of the type found all over the French capital, the sort of place where a man can sit for an evening over a Cassis or a cup of coffee and let the rest of the world go by. It was the place where, such a short time ago, Frank Matthews had received the package of heroin.

The old man who had given it to him had left the cafe and was now huddled in the doorway, wrapping his worn overcoat round him as he tried to stay out of the rain. As the car stopped, he moved forward to it, a half-skipping walk, the legacy of a wound received in the war when he had fought in the resistance, an honorable time in his life which he could now only remember with shame and sadness.

As he stood by the side of the car, Calmet wound down the window and favoured him with a thin, humourless smile. The old man peered myopically into the interior of the car:

"Please. My money?"

Calmet, his eyes hard and blank behind his spectacle lenses, made a gesture with his head towards the rear of the car, then leant forward so that the old man could see past him. The old man leaned his head right into the space left by the winding down of the window and looked towards the two rear passengers, the nervous greed which showed in his face freezing there as he saw the revolver held in Fortuit's hand, the barrel resting on the back of the front passenger seat, so that it was pointed unerringly at the centre of his forehead.

The old man got a split second to register Fortuit's tight smile, before the gunman squeezed the trigger. Fortuit laughed as he shot. This was a part of his work that he always enjoyed. It gave him the power he lacked in the rest of his life.

In spite of the sudden jerking-back of his head, a reflex of fear, the bullet passed almost exactly through the centre of the old man's forehead, killing him instantly and without a sound. The body fell against the side of the car, then to the ground as Kurt once more gunned the engine and the Citroen shot back to the entrance of the tiny cul-de-sac. He made a turn and the car went slowly away down the street into the rain and the blackness of the night. Still showing no outward sign of his emotions, Calmet inwardly relaxed. It had been a perfect operation, no one disturbed, no witnesses—no one left to provide a link with Jacques Brizard and the operation in Marseilles.

Though the car was gone, the street remained the same, silent and washed with the light autumn rain. Only to one person were other people arriving and he could see them because he was dying.

Rita and Kevin still stood in front of him, but they had been joined by a third figure who towered over them, dwarfing them and making Frank seem suddenly inadequate and helpless. He tried to speak again, to explain that he had made no errors, that his failure had been due entirely to coincidence, he could think of no other reason for it. Even as his numbed mind tried to form the words, he knew it was no use, Steve Ventura only wanted to hear about success, never failure, he did not accept failure from his operatives and they respected him for that; he never asked them to do anything that he had not done, or would not do, himself.

Frank had been so sure that the operation had been working, was convinced that he had been close to linking Brizard and Calmet in with the pushers of refined dope both in Europe and the United States. The package from the old man was the key that had locked that link into place. And now he was blown—at the critical moment Jacques Brizard had been warned, or had got on to him. But there was just no way that could have happened. As the thought receded, Frank Matthews used some of his last precious moments to figure out his mistake.

As he raised his head to speak, the three images seemed to fade away until all he could see was the wet cobbles shining in the street lamps, then they became a vague blur, then the blessed warm blackness overtook him. A moment later Frank Matthews, accredited Diplomat at the U.S. Embassy in Paris and a member of the office of the U.S. Dangerous Drugs Bureau, was dead.

Far away, on the outskirts of Paris, Calmet was dropped at a small railway halt from which he was due to catch the Express to Marseilles when it stopped for a mail pick up. He was the only man who would speak of that evening's work again—and then only to report to Jacques Brizard that Matthews had been eliminated and to repeat to him the last order he had given to the other three men:

"You must be back in Marseilles by the weekend. First, get Ventura."

Steve Ventura half-lay, half-sat in his rumpled bed, praying inwardly for a cigarette. He had given them up only a few days before, but his determination was becoming a little ragged round the edges. He pressed his leonine head against the bedhead and Rita Matthews paused in the repairs she was making to her hair to admire his deep barrel-chest and the rippling muscles of his shoulders. Every inch of him was still muscle. Fifteen years had made little difference to his physique and Rita Matthews was pleased as she combed her hair, and smiled at herself in the dressing mirror.

Steve turned to stare at her lean, strong frame. Rita Matthews had changed little more than her name in the last fifteen years. She was perhaps a little more rounded, there was a mark here and there which gave a clue to the fact that she had borne Frank Matthews a son in the intervening years, but she was still the Rita he remembered and had never been able to put out of his mind. As she became aware of her lover's scrutiny, she reddened with embarrassment and made as if to cover herself:

"What are you looking at? Are you sorry?"

Sorry? No, Steve wasn't sorry. The fact that her husband was somewhere out in the city on a dangerous undercover job gave him only the smallest twinge of guilt in this context. Frank had been gone for a month now, but it had only been tonight that he had succumbed to temptation and persuaded Rita to come back to his apartment. He had been worried when Matthews was assigned to him. He did not like the idea of him bringing Rita and their son Kevin to Paris, but Washington had arranged it without a murmur and who was he to question them. Rita had known that Steve Ventura would be her husband's boss in Paris, so, if she had no objection to coming, then there was no fair argument he could put against it. Steve smiled as he answered her question:

"Only you."

She blushed again:

"Why, have I changed that much?"

"Yeah, for the better." He swung himself off the bed and towered over her. Smiling, she put her arms round his neck and pressed herself close to him, feeling the warmth of his well-muscled frame, feeling him spring to renewed life. Her voice was husky.

"You want to know something. You're better too. Much better."

He tried to keep his voice light:

"That's nice to know."

They began to kiss with a warmth and passion that bridged the whole fifteen years of their separation. As they did so, Steve swung her round so that she fell back onto the bed. As he moved over her, she managed to break and roll away with an abrupt movement:

"Steve, please, not now. I'm sorry, but I promised the babysitter I'd be back by eleven. I must go."

With a light but patently false smile he moved away from her and began to dress:

"Okay, I'll take you."

Rita stood up and began to comb her hair again. Then changing her mind, she started to dress:

"Don't bother. I'm sure I'll be able to find a taxi at the corner. It'll be simpler that way."

Steve was too busy struggling with his socks to answer for a moment, then:

"Honey, it's no bother. My pleasure."

"You've had your pleasure," she laughed. "I'll find a cab."

"I'll drive you," he pleaded, almost like a child being deprived of a special treat. "I'd like to take you, to be with you. It's no bother."

When she turned to look him in the eye he knew

that he had said the wrong thing, the old anger he could remember was blazing in her eyes:

"You would too. You bastard, you wouldn't care if he saw us together in your car, would you?"

"But he won't—," Steve corrected himself hurriedly. "You said he wasn't expected home yet."

If she had noticed the slip—the reminder that Steve Ventura ran her husband's life, Rita gave no sign of it. When she spoke, her voice sounded a good deal more relaxed and he breathed an inward sigh of relief:

"I told you I've no idea when he's going to come home and you haven't either. With our luck it could just be tonight."

There was a silence between them as they finished dressing. As Steve slipped on his jacket, his eyes roved round his small apartment, looking everywhere except at her, as if trying to decide whether or not to ask something, delaying the decision on the question for as long as he could. At last:

"Look, Rita, we've got to talk about what's happened. We've got things to decide."

She snorted:

"You made the big decision a long time ago."

Steve could only shrug, there was no answer to that. In its way it was true enough, and yet too simple by far. There had been other pressures, other needs. When the moment had originally come for Steve and Rita to decide about themselves, life had been that much more precarious.

Steve had been CIA then, a field operative, working mainly in South America, at a time when every revolution was going to the left instead of the right for a change. In that game, Steve could only make one slip and there would have been a bullet waiting for him.

Rita had been a secretary in Washington then, she had known the risks he had been running. She had been more than willing to run the risk of being short of a husband at any moment, but Steve had still been young enough to want more for her than that.

It had taken a three-day drunk to work up the courage to tell her that he was going to walk away from her, and even then every word had been wrenched from him with almost physical pain. There had been women since then, plenty of women, but none of them had ever erased the memory of Rita from his mind—and this evening had renewed the love for her that he had always kept locked away deep within himself.

As he watched her finishing her make-up and preparing herself for the street, he tried to recall that last time they had been together, before she had screamed at him to get out and he had done just that—disappearing into an Asian turmoil for over a year.

When he had returned she was married to a junior operative, newly come to the service and on Washington assignment, Frank Matthews. At that time he faced nothing but a series of desk jobs, could never suspect he would ever face the dangers of the field and Steve remembered wishing them well.

He felt the irony of it all now—him a desk man instead of Frank, sending the latter out on field assignments as others had done to him in the old days. Rita cut across his thoughts:

"Steve, I'm sorry, but I really have to go."

He lumbered over to the peg by the door, took down her coat and helped her on with it:

"I'm sorry, Honey, listen, how are you fixed for tomorrow. Any chance that we can see each other."

Once more he sounded like a little boy and Rita smiled at the sound of such pleading coming from a man in his mid-forties, strong and self-sufficient, dependable and in control of everything that went on around him. She turned to face him, thinking hard, and the smile was replaced by a frown of genuine disappointment:

"I'm sorry—I have to take Kevin for a dental check and a friend's coming over for the evening. Thursday's out too—the hospital auxiliary. Maybe Friday, if Frank hasn't got back?"

It was Steve's turn to frown:

"Friday's never any good for me. I've got policy meetings at the Embassy all day."

Rita resisted the temptation to laugh out loud at the look of childish frustration that crossed his face. She had to bite her lip to fight it back before saying:

"The weekend's right out for me with Kevin. I guess that it'll have to be next week."

"Next week," he echoed forlornly.

She nodded and went to the door. Opening it, she turned back and managed a happy smile:

"Same time, same place?"

It took only two giant strides for him to be alongside her:

"And, thank God, the same girl."

He pressed her hard to him as if he wanted her to break. Then he let go with equal abruptness and stood back, closing the door gently on her retreating figure. For a moment he listened to the sound of her high heels clicking down the huge marble staircase which all old Parisian buildings seem to be equipped with, as she made for the only exit from the building.

He crossed quickly to the window and pulled aside the curtain to watch her come out into the street. The old block straddled the end of a cul-de-sac that spilled out into the main road. Backed as it was by the black walls of some huge modern office development, Steve had deliberately picked this location for his apartment. With only one entrance to cover it made security easier for him. From his window he could get a clear view of both pavements to the main road. No one could pay him a surprise visit if he was on the look-out. It was not selected for any pressing reason—just an example of Steve's perfect sense of the inherent dangers in his work.

At the end of the road was a small cafe, the sort that dot nearly every street corner in Paris. For most of the night, its lighted window illuminated the end of the street and, as Rita came out of the building and began to walk briskly towards the corner, Steve noticed that a man was standing outside the cafe, apparently waiting for something.

Steve felt the knot of tension in his gut. Rita walked briskly down the pavement, past the man, then raised her arm as she saw a taxi and hailed it. She got in and sped away, out of his line of vision. The man had not moved beyond giving her a casual glance. Perhaps he was just a lonely man standing in the rain.

Steve watched him for a moment more, then let the curtain fall back into place. He turned to the phone, lifted the receiver and dialled the number of the night watcher at the Embassy:

"Ventura here."

"Yes, Sir."

"Has Matthews made his report call?"

"No word from him yet, Sir."

Steve glanced at his watch. It read twenty minutes after eleven. He snapped:

"What time is he due to report in?"

"Eleven, Sir, but he's often up to ten or fifteen minutes late."

Steve made himself relax. He knew he was edgy, but Frank's assignment was important to him:

"Okay. No need to hit the panic button yet. But please call me as soon as he calls in. I'm at my apartment."

He gave the number and dropped the phone. He could still feel the little ball of tension in the pit of his stomach. He sensed that something was wrong, but could not quite put his finger on it. There was no reason to suppose that the operation had fouled up so, with a shrug, he put it down to feelings of guilt over his evening with Rita.

In the next hour, Steve finished off a couple of cans of beer, padding round, clearing up the apartment, as he waited for the call back, thinking all the time about Rita.

No, fifteen years had certainly not changed her, except for the better. Steve could feel himself beginning to ache for her again, in spite of his recent bout of love-making and he became impatient for the week to pass. Even as he thought of this the thought changed to worry about Frank's call. It should have come in by now.

Nothing was easy when you were up against Brizard, but the operation had been well-planned. Frank had been flown to Montreal, equipped with the false papers of a French-Canadian seaman and had worked his passage back to Marseilles and thus to his first drug contacts. He could either be back in Marseilles, or in Paris where he reported he had come the day before to do a little job for some pushers he had contacted, men that Ventura was sure were used by Brizard for a portion of his distribution network.

Still Brizard's security system was uncannily accurate. Six dead agents in two years were proof of that. Operations that came within a hairbreadth of involving him were suddenly snuffed out as if he had known of them all along. But Matthews wasn't supposed to get that close. Steve had planned to pull him out as a decoy as soon as he judged the moment to be right. . . .

Steve's head jerked up as the phone rang. As he

reached for the receiver he glanced at his watch. It was five in the morning and he had slept where he had sat, in a comfortable chair—a misnomer for the stiffness that he now felt.

"Hello."

It was the night watch at the Embassy:

"Mr. Ventura. There's been no call in from Mr. Matthews."

Steve suppressed a desire to curse the man for waking him to tell him nothing, and said:

"Okay, thanks for letting me know. I'll be right in. Inform anyone who has to know."

At least, he thought, as he slammed down the phone, the boy had had the sense to ring back. And he gave himself the small glimmer of satisfaction of knowing that the order he had given would include disturbing the night's rest of the Consular chief at the Embassy, Fred Williams, a man who always sneered at Steve and his operations and had shoved him and his secretary into one of the most uncomfortable offices in the Embassy.

He dressed hurriedly and was almost ready to leave when the phone rang again:

"Any word."

There was a silence at the other end, then a familiar French voice came down the phone:

"What would you like news about."

Steve stiffened, now really aware that something was wrong. For what other reason would Chief Inspector Briac of the Sureté be calling him personally at half past five in the morning:

"Hello, Briac, to what do I owe this pleasure?"

The Frenchman's voice was grim as he replied:

"I think we've got your man Matthews."

"Where?" The question was unnecessary. Steve felt

he knew the answer even as he asked the question. Briac's next words confirmed his fear:

"At the morgue, Matthews and another man."

It was a moment before Steve's voice was steady enough to ask the identity of the other man.

Briac gave an equally significant pause, then:

"We don't have the identification yet. Can you come down. No hurry, but I'm going to need you for a formal identification."

"Yeah," Steve glanced at his watch. "I'll be there at nine. Mind if I bring Kovakian with me."

Kovakian was the man who acted as Steve's assistant in the section.

"Right, see you at nine." With no goodbye, Briac cut the connection. He had obviously had a heavy, sleepless night. Steve picked up the phone again and called Kovakian's number. When the man answered, he used no preliminaries:

"Panic button. I'll pick you up in an hour."

"What happened, Steve."

"They wasted Matthews. We've got to talk before we go to the morgue."

He slammed down the receiver. As he stood up, and stretched the stiffness of the night in the chair from him, he was filled with a black rage. That bastard Brizard, sitting in his villa overlooking the Mediterranean and giving orders that snuffed out men's lives like candles, surrounded by an apparently impenetrable wall of thugs and political influence, the spider at the centre of one of the world's biggest narcotics operations, and no one seemed able to lay a finger on him, or come within yards of trying.

And now another man had been wasted, a man whose loss hit harder than most, partly because he was a good operative, and partly because Steve had spent that night with the man's wife, probably at just the time he was being killed.

It was only then that Steve remembered to call back the Embassy. They wouldn't have to call Fred Williams from his bed after all—though he half-hoped they had been efficient just this once and had done so already.

They went in Kovakian's car to the morgue. Steve did not trust himself at the wheel with the anger that was burning him up at the thought of Frank's death. They were still ten minutes ahead of time when Kovakian parked the car in the yard that fronted on to the building, but Inspector Briac was already waiting for them on the steps. A career police officer of the generation that had entered the Sureté after the war, Chief Inspector Briac, though only about five years younger than Steve Ventura, still retained a peculiarly gallic youthful charm.

As he walked towards the car, Steve noted with a certain irritation that he seemed freshly shaven and gave no sign that he had been up most of the night.

He shook hands with the two men, then walked with them to the building. Steve muttered:

"Is there any chance. . . ."

"I'm sorry," said Briac softly. "It's Matthews. I knew him remember."

The three men walked in silence down the rubber-floored, white-walled corridor and into the blazing neon of the room where the newly-dead were kept, each in their separate cold cabinet, waiting identification or post-mortem.

A silent, white-coated technician was waiting for them and Briac handed him a card on which was written the numbers of the two corpses he wanted to view.

The man slid out a drawer. Inside lay the body of a man completely swathed in a white sheet.

Briac beckoned Steve forward with him, leant over the corpse and expertly moved the sheets so that the white, drained face was exposed to view. Steve had seen many corpses, some of those he knew, some of those he did not know, but on this occasion he came as close to flinching and turning away as he had ever done. Briac gave him a moment, then cleared his throat:

"Mr. Ventura, just for the record you understand; is that Frank Matthews?"

Steve swallowed and did not answer for a moment. Inside him the one chance, the one slight hope that a mistake had been made, was dead. Briac repeated:

"Is that Frank Matthews?"

Steve took a deep breath, the word rasping in his throat:

"Yes."

Briac nodded his thanks and moved forward to where the technician was sliding out a second drawer in his macabre wall collection. Kovakian looked down at the face of the second corpse and Steve followed Briac over, happy to get away from the imagined accusation on Frank's dead face. The three observers saw an elderly man, peaceful in death, with a small hole drilled almost exactly in the centre of his forehead above the bridge of his nose:

"Do you know this man, Mr. Kovakian?"

Kovakian and Steve frowned down at the face of the old stranger. Kovakian shook his head:

"I've never seen him before."

Briac turned to Steve:

"How about you."

"Never. When you spoke to me, you didn't know who he was either. Did you get a trace on him?"

Briac nodded and smiled.

"We found him in records. His name is Charles Vilmette. He was a cog in the Resistance, then after the war he took to petty crime, you know the sort of thing."

He stopped speaking and Steve shrugged and turned away. But Briac was saving the important piece of information until the last:

"He comes from Marseilles."

In the emotional atmosphere of the morgue, Steve, his thoughts filled with guilt at Frank's death and his night with Rita Matthews, was caught off guard. He stiffened and turned back to face the policeman. It was only a momentary lapse and he managed to recover himself:

"Of course I would have no way of knowing him. I have never been to Marseilles."

He was irritated by the return of Briac's smile and turned away to leave:

"Mr. Ventura. There are still some questions I would like to ask you."

Steve contained his anger:

"Mr. Briac, do they have to be right now?"

Briac shook his head, but he was no longer smiling:

"No, when would be a convenient time?"

Steve gave it a moment's thought. He would want to see Rita, do a report for the office, see if the implications of co-operating with the Sureté would infringe any of the jealously-guarded rights of diplomatic immunity which the Embassy staff were forced, by the current Ambassador, to obey to the letter. At last, he said:

"Let's make it six-thirty tonight. At the Raphael Bar."

Briac nodded his agreement and farewell.

Steve walked quickly back down the corridor, his shoes squealing on the rubber floor. He was in the open air, pausing to wish he had a cigarette, before Kovakian caught up with him. Steve turned to speak to him, then clamped his mouth shut as Briac appeared behind them:

"By the way, your friend Matthews. He was married?"

"Yes?"

"Do you want me to give the news to his wife?"

Steve felt warmer towards the policeman. He managed a thin smile of thanks as he answered:

"No, I'll tell her."

Briac nodded and turned back into the building. It was only after the door had closed on him that Kovakian blurted:

"Steve. I can read you like a book. You know who killed Frank Matthews, don't you?"

They walked together towards the car:

"I've a pretty good idea, Joe."

"That's two operatives in a row. Why can't we just make Brizard disappear—a nice quiet job."

Steve was genuinely surprised and puzzled to find himself a little shocked by the suggestion. He turned to Kovakian, a frown crossing his brow:

"Like how?"

"Like kill him," shrugged Kovakian.

"But that's against the law, Joe." The unconscious irony of his remark was lost on Kovakian, who lit a cigarette under Steve's envious eye before replying:

"It could be the only way."

They walked to the car in silence, each wrapped in his own thoughts concerning Frank Matthews' death and the culpability of Jacques Brizard. Opening the door, Kovakian threw away his cigarette and Steve watched it burn on the cobbles of the yard:

"Listen, Steve, I have to get to the Embassy. Reports and formal notification will have to be made. Can I give you a lift?"

Steve shook his head:

"I'd better go see Rita—Matthews. Tell my girl I'll report in later, will you."

Kovakian watched as he walked to the gateway and turned down the street, his head bent, his brow furrowed with thought. As he walked he tried to put out of his mind the coming ordeal of telling Rita Matthews that her husband was dead—had died during the night, perhaps while they had been making love. Instead he thought of Joe Kovakian's suggestion—the tiny seed that he had planted in Steve's mind, which was already taking tenacious root.

Make Jacques Brizard disappear. It was a tempting suggestion.

CHAPTER TWO

Steve had lost count of the number of times he had walked to the living room window of the Matthews apartment and looked out at the blustery sky. Kevin, at nine already equipped with the blood-thirsty instincts of boys twice his age, was using the floor of the room for some obscurely-complicated war game. His particular pride and joy was a toy tank which clicked its way across the carpet and polished parquet, but which required innumerable re-windings, always accompanied by blood-curdling imitations of dive-bombing and machine gun fire.

Steve was happy that the boy was wrapped up in his game and taking little notice of him as he could not bring himself to face the boy's questions.

When he had arrived at the apartment and had rung the bell, the door had been opened a fraction by Kevin, carefully keeping it on the chain, who announced that his Mother was out shopping. On seeing Steve he had delightedly let him in, only to upset the man by asking:

"Uncle Steve, when's Daddy coming home?"

Steve had muttered that he didn't know and had

been subjected to a scrutiny which made him squirm with discomfort. Relief only came when the boy decided to turn his attention back to the game he had been playing when Steve arrived.

Somehow, the tank became entangled with his legs and Steve turned away from the window once again only to trip over Kevin:

"Have you any idea where your Mother went? It's been nearly an hour."

"She'll be back soon," frowned Kevin, rewinding the tank with deep concentration.

Steve looked down at him, feeling an almost overwhelming impulse to take the boy up in his arms, to tell him about his father and to comfort him. This was the son that he and Rita might have had if only. . . .

He cut off the train of thought abruptly as he heard a key turn in the lock. She came in without glancing in his direction, her arms filled with packages, slamming the door expertly behind her with her foot and calling for her son at the same time. As the boy ran to her, she stumbled into the living room and let the packages tumble onto the large polished table at its centre. It was only then that she saw Steve staring at her, standing guiltily by the window:

"What the hell are you doing here?"

Steve could feel the speech he had been practising with one corner of his mind ebb into forgotten limbo. He clenched and unclenched his fists:

"I-I had to see you."

They both glanced at Kevin as if seeing him between them for the first time. Rita shook her head brusquely at Steve, then picked up one of the packages:

"Kevin, darling, will you take this laundry into Mummy's bedroom."

Kevin, aware with the innocence of a child, that his

elders were about to embark on some conversation that he was not to hear, glanced wickedly at the two faces above him, then sensing the tension between them, he snatched the package and ran from the room.

Rita bent down, picked up the tank and placed it on the table. It started to move forward, the sound of the clockwork cutting across the heavy silence and causing her to jump. She snatched at it and stopped it:

"These damned toys."

"Rita, please, this isn't easy."

She turned on him:

"You're damned right it isn't. What the hell do you mean by it. I told you you couldn't come here."

Steve put out his hands in a helpless gesture, too overcome to speak for a moment, as if he was trying to push her anger away:

"There's—there's something—."

He broke off abruptly as Kevin came back into the room, his errand run at double speed. He went straight for his tank, but Rita got her hand to it first:

"Kevin—tell you what—why don't you go along the corridor to Jean-Claude. He might like to go out and play."

Kevin scuffed one shoe against the other:

"But, Mom, he doesn't even speak English."

Rita snapped:

"Listen, you're in his country, you should learn to speak his language. Now, don't argue. Hurry up."

They both watched Kevin trot reluctantly to the door and waited until it closed behind him, one last pleading glance producing no softening in his mother's attitude. Rita turned back to Steve with a shrug of resignation:

"Alright, what's done is done. Now what's so important that it couldn't wait—hang on, sit down for a minute and I'll make some coffee."

Steve could stand the delay no longer. As she turned, he stepped forward and grabbed her by the wrist. Rita cried out with the pain, but he held her still as he blurted:

"Please—I have to tell you—last night—Frank was killed."

Her whole body tensed and he let go and stepped back. Rita stood quite still, staring at him, her eyes blank as if she was refusing to take in the information. When she spoke, her voice was dull and even, giving no sign of her inner feelings:

"I'll go make the coffee."

She walked quickly to the kitchen and out of sight. A moment later came the crash of falling crockery and a cry:

"Oh, my God."

Steve ran into the kitchen. Rita was standing, grasping the edge of the sink, her knuckles white, the tears flowing as she acknowledged the death of her husband. He took her roughly in his arms and squeezed her tightly to him, trying to hold her mind as well as her body, shield her somehow from the pain:

"Rita, honey, I'm sorry, baby, I'm sorry."

For an eternity, she remained in his arms, sobbing quietly on his shoulder. As she stepped back at last she said, her voice barely under control:

"Kevin. I have to tell him. How am I going to tell him?"

Steve's voice was gentle:

"I'll tell him."

"No."

"He doesn't know anything. It'll be best."

She nodded absently, her thoughts racing on:

"How did it happen?"

"He-He was crushed by a car."

"Was it—was it because of us?"

"No. It had nothing to do with us."

He followed her back into the living room. She sat down, staring at the pattern on the carpet in front of her:

"I don't know what to do. Please, really I don't."

Steve squeezed her shoulder:

"If you want to, just cry."

He stood for a long time, looking down at her, wishing that he could heal her suffering, trying to assuage his own guilt. If it had not been for him, Frank Matthews would still be alive. And all the time, Kovakian's casual words at the morgue whirled round in his brain. Getting rid of Brizard outside the law was still only a wild suggestion, but it was gaining ground in his hurt, angry mind with every moment that passed.

Afterwards, Steve Ventura could not remember how he had spent the rest of that day. He left Rita only when he was sure that she was recovered enough from her shock to be under control. He had found Kevin and had told him. The boy had kicked and screamed at him as thanks for his compassion.

For the rest of the day he walked through the damp, windy city and it was only by apparent chance that his footsteps led him to the Hotel Raphael and the bar shortly after six o'clock.

As he entered he made the wrenching effort needed to take his mind away from his inner pain and back to his more pressing problems. He blinked round the dimly-lit bar, then saw Briac waving to him from one of the polished-wood booths at the far end. He walked over and saw that the detective was equipped with a bottle of wine and two glasses:

"Sorry I'm late. I ran into a little problem."

Briac, who made it his business to be informed of every move Steve Ventura made, shook his hand:

"Problem?"

The telephone report a few minutes before had told him that Steve had walked directly from the morgue to Rita Matthews' apartment. He had remained inside for the rest of the morning, and, when he had left, had commenced a laborious walking tour of the city. He had neither eaten, nor made any telephone calls. Steve said:

"It's nothing—you said that you had some questions for me?"

"Yes—but you must have a drink—wine?"

Steve shook his head:

"I'll have a bourbon on the rocks."

Briac disappeared to the bar and returned a few moments later, carrying the drink. Steve thanked him and took a long swig. Briac reseated himself, facing the American:

"I'm sorry, but I need some information on Matthews."

Steve adopted his poker face:

"I'm sure you know as much as I do."

Briac nodded, finished his glass of wine and poured another. He smiled his most charming smile in an attempt to defuse the tension he felt was mounting across the table:

"It's a very good wine."

Steve glared at him, then felt in his pockets. He produced a battered pack of Gauloise and put one in his mouth. Briac was instantly at the ready with his lighter, but Steve waved it away:

"No, thanks. I've given it up." At the frown that crossed Briac's face, he elaborated: "It helps, sucking them. I'll lose the taste in the end."

Briac smiled for a moment, then assumed a serious expression:

"Mr. Ventura. Let's drop all this. You are a policeman and so am I. Why don't we help each other by pooling what we know."

"Okay," growled Steve. "You tell me what you know first."

Briac hesitated, but only for a moment. He realised that Steve was not bluffing, would admit nothing without some concessions first:

"All we know for sure is that Frank Matthews was working for the U.S. Bureau of Narcotics and Dangerous Drugs. You are in charge of the Paris office. You came here to take over last year."

"August," agreed Steve.

"Yes, August the second. Before that, one of our men came across you during an operation in Istanbul two years ago."

Steve smiled expansively:

"You've certainly done your homework."

Briac changed tack abruptly:

"Tell me, why was Frank Matthews carrying a false Canadian passport and seaman's card when he was found—and this photograph?"

He took a small snapshot from his top pocket and slid it across the table. Steve peered at the blurred features of Jacques Brizard taken with a telephoto lens climbing out his car. Apart from the area of his face obscured by a large pair of dark glasses it was not a bad likeness:

"He was posing as a seaman from Quebec."

Briac frowned:

"Quebec—why Quebec?"

"They speak French in Quebec."

Briac's pleasure at the answer was relaxed and genuine:

"Of course. It is always the simple, obvious explanations that get missed—but why that photograph?"

Steve hesitated, studying the Frenchman's face. He

was taking stock, looking for an answer in his features, pondering whether or not it would be right to trust this man. A straight cop was a rarity in any country these days, but Briac seemed on the up and up. Steve decided to trust him:

"He's been in Marseilles trying to get evidence against Jacques Brizard on some of his operations—drug-running mainly."

The answer seemed to hit a nerve in the detective. He abandoned any attempt at cool interest and leant forward earnestly:

"And—?"

Steve shrugged:

"I'm afraid he was killed before he could report anything of value to us. But he must have found something, got somewhere—or why would Brizard have him eliminated."

"Do you have any proof at all?"

Steve looked steadily at the bright eyes of the detective. He asked his question with concentrated deliberation:

"Tell me, if I could bring you the proof that was needed, would you have Jacques Brizard arrested and put in jail?"

Briac shrugged:

"You know that it would be up to the examining magistrate and the courts."

It was a better answer than he had expected, but they were all the same in the end, afraid of authority, afraid of crossing the line that brought them up against a political wall, power that influenced their careers and futures; and the men on both sides of the law who wielded such power:

"Forget I asked."

Briac sighed:

"Believe me, I know what you are thinking. I admit,

it is very difficult—a delicate situation. Jacques Brizard is, how would you put it, is a very private individual, well guarded both personally and politically. It makes us very wary of acting as we might choose to under fairer circumstances. You must have absolute proof to move against a man like that at all—surely, you can understand that?"

"He also controls the courts, I have no doubt, if the worst ever came to the worst?"

"I wouldn't go that far."

Steve sighed:

"It's a problem. He's some kind of untouchable, isn't he?"

"One could call him that. As for me, I prefer to say that he leads a charmed life."

"So did my cat, until somebody killed him," snapped Steve. He threw down the cigarette he had been chewing and absent-mindedly took a replacement from the pack that Briac had left on the table, patting his pockets for a light, ignoring the detective's lighter. The other man watched this display of nerves with only the slightest hint of detached amusement:

"I am sorry about your cat. But to get back to Monsieur Brizard. He is the sort of man who might have you killed—if you invaded his privacy."

Steve rose abruptly:

"Which leads us right back to Frank Matthews. Listen, if you don't have any more questions, I have another appointment to get to."

The detective shook his head:

"No, nothing for the moment."

Steve nodded, thanked the man for the drink, then slid out of the booth. Briac was still staring thoughtfully at his retreating back, when he whirled round, remembering something, and came back to the table. He was smiling:

"By the way, you've got it a bit wrong. It was Frank Matthews who was in Instambul—I was running things in Mexico City."

If he had hoped to push the detective off-balance, he failed. The other man merely shrugged and said:

"Thank you. I'll have the relevant information re-docketed on the files."

Steve shook the detective warmly by the hand:

"Never mind. Nobody's perfect, not even Sureté records. I'm sure I'll see you around."

"I'm sure."

Steve Ventura had only one appointment that night—to crawl into a whiskey bottle. He sat in the dark in his apartment, toasting the memory of Frank Matthews and trying to drown the pricking of his conscience over his colleague's death. It was a strange irony to him that if Frank was alive, he would have no conscience at all about his night with Rita. But with Frank dead, he knew he would have to take some decisive action to make the balance sheet even.

It was late, and he was very drunk when he tried to call Rita to babble renewed apologies and beg the chance to go round to her, but there was no reply to his ring. Perhaps she had gone to stay with friends. He felt profoundly relieved that there had been no reply.

He woke with the bustle of the day floating through his open windows, lying face down on the bed, still fully clothed and with a king-sized hangover.

Somehow he got himself together enough to excite no unfavourable comment from the Embassy staff who saw him as he went to his office. He shouted at Sally, his secretary, that he wasn't taking any calls. The tiny office was another sanctum, a womb in which to hide, as was his apartment. Cached in various odd corners was a good stock of Bourbon and Steve settled down to a day of steady drinking. The punishment he had given himself the night before took the edge off the liquor and it no longer had any euphoric effect.

It was nearly the end of the day when Sally took her life in her hands and decided to disturb him. She was a tall, rangy girl, who hailed from Nebraska and had been lured abroad by the thought of foreign travel. Ten years in various parts of the world had taught her that people are very much the same wherever you go—but she liked Steve Ventura more than most. She had a trim figure, nothing spectacular, but nothing she worried about and a face that had often been described as 'neat'. She had never been able to figure out quite what that meant, but knew that if she was not Raquel Welch, she wasn't Boris Karloff either.

The desk bore witness to Steve's activities during the day. There was one empty whiskey bottle, and one near empty one. A glass stood between them. Steve had swivelled his chair round and was staring sightlessly out of the window at the grey sky, the only splash of colour made by the American flag hanging limply in the line of sight of the window.

Sally cleared her throat nervously as she walked over to the desk:

"Steve—Uh—Mr. Ventura. It's getting almost to get up and go time—you want to know who called?"

Steve spun round:

"Shoot."

Sally Weinberg never forgot a detail—that was one reason why Steve was happy to employ her:

"Bowman, Evans, Jacobs, Jones, Henshaw and, last but not least, the ever-persistent Joe Kovakian, who will, as always, try you again later."

Steve turned his chair so that he had his back to her again:

"Nobody else."

Sally sighed:

"No, she didn't call."

Steve groped for his glass, drained it, then poured the remains of the second bottle into it before taking another swift gulp. He glanced round, then snapped:

"Wasn't there another bottle of this stuff round here someplace?"

"It's in the bottom right hand drawer of the desk."

She watched him snatch open the drawer, withdraw the full bottle and unscrew the cap. He poured some into his half empty glass as she leant across the desk, worry showing in her face:

"Steve, why don't you come over to my place and let me cook you dinner. Anything would be better than this."

"No." He slammed down his fist, but she was unabashed.

"Why not?"

He grinned up at her malevolently:

"Because you're such a goddam lousy cook—besides this is my main course for the moment."

Sally retreated, knowing when she was beaten:

"I think you'll find you have another glass in the bottom left hand drawer."

He blinked up at her as the hint sunk in, then found the glass and handed it to her. She held it out as he poured in a generous measure of liquor:

"Be my guest."

They both clinked glasses and drank in silence, Steve glancing away at the lowering sky. Sally found her courage:

"When the hell are you going to stop third degreeing yourself?"

"What do you mean?"

Sally took another swig to bolster up her courage. Off and on she had known Steve Ventura as a boss, an operative, and a lover for five years. She did not reproach herself for having succumbed to him, he had never taken what was not on eager offer. He had bouts of destructive depression when he took to the bottle, but she had never seen him in such a self-destructive mood as now:

"Look, we've known each other a long time, right?"

"So?"

"Well, Steve Ventura, I can read you like a book."

"Don't tell me the end of the story," he snapped, holding up his hand for her to stop talking, but Sally was too screwed up to stop now:

"Why don't you tell me what's really bugging you about all this. It isn't just Frank getting killed, is it?"

He looked up at her in silence and, in that moment, she guessed what had happened. She began to wish she had kept her mouth shut. Steve stood up and thumped his glass down on the desk:

"You want to know. You really want to know." She jumped back as he swept his hand round the small office and looked as if he might reach across and hit her: "It's this Goddam office, that's what's really bugging me—but most of all, I hate this Goddam desk. I should have objected. I should have stayed out in the field when I had the chance. That's where I belong."

He stood by the window, staring into the gloom of dusk in a morose silence, wrapped in a pall of regrets. Sally said softly:

"It's even rougher out there."

"Maybe, but they get the job done. It's men like Frank Matthews who really close down on the pushers and peddlers, not desk jockeys like me."

"Look what happened to Frank."

She felt uncomfortable as his face changed from anger to shame as he realised that he had been wallowing in self-pity; that he had taken Frank's death as a personal slap in the face, not an operational failure. His voice was quiet:

"Sally, what has happened to me? What's going on? I used to like what I was doing."

"Join the club. A lot of us feel the same way."

"Then why did I take this desk job. What am I doing here?"

Sally shrugged:

"Your job is what you're doing. Face up to it. You're head of the Paris office, the most important station outside the Western Hemisphere, the centre of everything you're trying to stop—accept it."

Steve shook his head:

"I can't. I give orders and other people die. I just can't."

He was still, then, growling under his breath, he pushed past her and stormed out of his office and along the corridor. Sally sighed. That meant trouble for somebody—most probably Fred Williams, the liaison between the main Embassy and the specialised officers. Still, Thursday was Fred's special day out of the office. Sally looked at her watch. With any luck she could be out of harm's way and in the Metro before Steve came back. If she was going to go home, there was no time like the present.

As for Steve, Sally had read the result of his actions like a clairvoyant. Fred Williams had the biggest office and the prettiest secretary in the building. As with all the laws of the civil service, it followed that he spent less time in his office than anyone else—Thursdays particularly.

Janet was rushing the last of her typing before going home for the day as Steve stormed in:

"Hiya, Janet, I'm going in for a word with Fred."

Instinctively, she stood to bar his way:

"Mr. Ventura, I'm afraid that Mr. Williams isn't in."

The look he gave her, Janet wished the floor would open and swallow her up. Pad clutched in one hand, pencil in the other, she wished she had never stood up. She made a conscious effort to keep her voice steady:

"May I take a message?"

"I just want to say three little words to him."

She began to wilt visibly:

"He's really not in, Mr. Ventura."

"Where is he?"

She did her best:

"He's keeping the same appointment he has every Thursday afternoon. I'm not going to disturb him there."

"Which suite?"

"Three oh six." She cursed inwardly as she gave the location of her boss's poker session away. The whole Embassy knew the only hotel he would play in was the Raphael. He swung away from her and had his hand on the door when she called:

"Oh, Mr. Ventura, you never gave me the message—the three little words."

Steve turned and grimaced:

"The first one is go—."

She was writing it down carefully when the door slammed behind him.

Fred Williams was a career diplomat who had been with the Embassy in Paris for far longer than the normal tour of duty. He had first arrived in the French capital some seven years before and had liked what he had found there—a bustling social circle of expatriate Americans—with a few Englishmen thrown in, for they did, after all, speak the same language.

He was no mean organiser, so he had built a comfortable niche for himself at the Embassy, one which, amongst other comforting details, gave him as little contact as possible with the French. He might have been spending his days in the New York he came from and loved so well.

With a group of friends, he had started a regular poker school which met every Thursday after lunch in a suite at the Raphael Hotel and whose earnest meetings would sometimes go on until well after the opening of Embassy business on Friday mornings. Everyone at the Embassy knew that Fred's Thursdays were sacrosanct and interrupted them at their peril. The visit of an important American to Paris, such as a President, who would occupy Fred's Thursdays with other matters, caused a wave of fear to pass through the Embassy, for Fred would be out of sorts for weeks.

This Thursday was no exception to Fred's rules and he was holed up in suite 306 losing his shirt to four of his compatriots; James Jones, Gene Moskowitz, Alan Rossett and Bill Kearns, while Sam White, the brilliant Paris correspondent of the London Evening Standard took time out on the couch in the corner.

Even Steve, angry though he was, paused for a moment to collect his momentum before entering the room, instinctively blinking in the gloom. The air was thickened by a cloud of cigar smoke—Fred was on his favorite Monte Cristos:

"Hi Fred."

Fred Williams frowned as he recognised the voice, but did not look up:

"Hi, Steve."

"Dealer takes three," snapped Kearns.

Steve leant between Kearns and Fred, breathing alcoholically on the latter's cards:

"Fred, I have to talk to you."

Fred placed his hands over his paunch, to hide his cards and wrinkled his nose at the smell of stale alcohol:

"Steve, please, not now. Not in the middle of a poker game."

"It'll cost you a hundred," said Jones, carrying on the bidding.

"Yes, now. It's important."

"Call it," said Kearns. Then: "Hey, fellah, do you mind knocking it off. We're trying to play cards here. Fred, are you in or out. I already called."

It took a major effort for Steve to contain himself. He saw that the only way to get Fred's attention would be to play his game for him, for, truth be told, Fred Williams was a rotten poker player. He glanced at the cards, then snatched Fred's money:

"We raise you two fifty."

Fred glared at him, then gave up the unequal struggle while trying to maintain the fiction that he was running his own betting:

"Yeah, we raise you two fifty."

The other players digested the heavy bet and rechecked their cards. Steve said:

"Fred, do you know I hate my desk?"

"Goddam it, Steve, if that's all that's bothering you, I'll move you in a new desk—now are you guys going to call or raise or what?"

One by one the other players dropped out, leaving only Kearns, the dealer, still holding his cards. He inspected them with deep concentration for a while, then threw them down in disgust:

"We seem to be moving furniture rather than playing cards. I'm out."

Steve scraped the money up in front of Fred:

"You bluffed them. It's a hell of a pot."

"Whose deal?"

"It's mine," answered Fred, reaching for the cards. Steve grabbed his arm and held it in a vice-like grip. His voice was urgent, almost whining in his plea:

"Stay out the next one will you please. I have to talk to you, it's important."

"Can't we take this damned thing up at the office in the morning?"

"Oh. come on, Fred. This is really important. I wouldn't have barged in here if—"

Kearns cut across him, growling:

"Why don't you two guys go into the bedroom—it's nice and quiet—for us as well."

Fred glanced round the table and the aggressive faces of his fellow-players echoed Kearns' request. He rose with bad grace and waddled across the room to the door to the bedroom, Steve following in his wake. The two men were the same age but presented a striking contrast, Steve all bone and muscle, Fred Williams all fat. As Steve crossed the threshold to the other room, he heard Kearns mutter:

"He doesn't like his desk, Jeez."

Fred swung round to see the look on Steve's face and quickly shut the door so that he could not go back and start a fight:

"Now, what the hell is all this about, Steve?"

"Fred, I really hate my desk."

The latter moved back to the door:

"Well, you wanna know something, Steve. I hate my desk too and I'm going right back out there to play a little poker."

Steve barred his way, on the edge of going out of control. He was shaking with anger:

"Wait a minute, Fred, you have to listen to me. I want a clearance from you—a big favour. Let me go out after Jacques Brizard, please, Fred."

There was a long silence between the two men. Fred was suddenly grim, realising the fight that was going on inside his colleague. He hadn't liked Frank Matthews' death one little bit. Perhaps, in similar circumstances, running a man who was wasted by the enemy, he might have felt the same. But it was not a time for emotion and when he looked at Steve, his face and voice were grim:

"You know I can't do that, Steve."

Steve put his hands on the other man's shoulders as if wanting the need for revenge to flow from him into Fred:

"First there was Ed Marcus, right? And now Frank Matthews has been killed, right? You know as well as I do that Brizard had them killed because they were getting close to linking him in with the drug operations."

"But Steve, you know you can't prove that Brizard had them killed and opinion isn't enough. He's an important national in a country where we are guests. Our hands are tied. You'd have to have positive proof."

"You get me off this office hook and let me go down to Marseilles and I'll bring back the proof."

"No," snarled Fred. "I expressly forbid it. You can't go."

In an agony of frustration, Steve slammed his fist into the thin door of the bedroom:

"Who in hell's name does he have to kill before we can go out after him in the open—does he have to knock off the whole Goddam bureau. Say, that's not a bad idea. If he does that, can I go after him?"

Kearns' voice was muffled by the woodwork, but he had a powerful pair of lungs:

"Why don't you two guys shut up."

Steve turned and shouted through the door:

"Fungoo." He slammed it again with his fist, then spun round as Fred caught his arm with all the strength he could muster. The senior man was in a bad temper now, red in the face, his cigar dropped on the floor and forgotten:

"Now Steve, let's get a couple of Goddam things straight before we go any further with this Brizard thing. Six months ago the French Foreign office called us in and lodged a formal complaint against your department—and you know what they said."

"Yeah."

"They said that you and your operatives were harassing a prominent French citizen. I told you then that you had to lay off Jacques Brizard—and what did you do as soon as the heat was off? You sent Frank Matthews down there on his tail. Look, Steve, I don't make the Goddam rules. I'm just here to see that they're obeyed. If Brizard disappeared tomorrow and was never seen again, I'd applaud as loud as the next man."

Steve frowned. Perhaps Fred was right. Perhaps Kovakian's way was the way to get rid of Brizard. He growled:

"That means I have to stick with my Goddam desk?"

Fred relaxed, he seemed to be getting through to his unreasoning colleague:

"You'd better believe it, Friend. And you lay off Jacques Brizard in future or you'll be transferred out of here so fast that your butt won't feel the seat of the plane."

He realised his mistake as soon as he had spoken. To Steve, threats from his own people were worse than a red rag to a bull:

"Is it threats now, Fred?"

Fred shook his head, trying to relax, bring the emotional temperature down a few degrees:

"Now look, Steve, let me be a pal. You've got a great deal. There's no need for anyone to rock the boat. You've got a good salary, a good job, and you've got department seniority. You've got a good expense account—and then you've got the discretionary secret fund—you can spend up to one hundred thousand dollars out of it without authorisation."

Steve bridled:

"And let's not forget the pension plan."

"Don't you Goddam forget the pension plan," snarled Fred. He turned away, opened the door and strode out of the room, to show the meeting was at an end as far as he was concerned. Steve followed, shouting as he went:

"Well, thanks a bunch for the Goddam lecture, Fred."

Ignoring him, Williams went back to his place at the poker table and glared round at the other players in turn. Steve swept past him, making for the door. As his hand went to it, to throw it back and leave, one of the other players growled:

"Goodbye, Fungoo."

Steve allowed his hand to drop back from the handle, spun round with a violence that made the men jump and walked back so that he was standing over the table, glaring down at them:

"Who spoke?"

It was Kearns who turned to face him, the trace of a defiant smile on his lips:

"I did. You want to make something out of it?"

Steve walked to him and thrust his face forward until it was only inches from the other man's. The atmosphere in the room became electric as the others waited to see what would happen. Steve Ventura was like a bomb, primed and ready to explode in their midst. The shout, when it came, caused Kearns to shift his chair backwards with a jerk:

"Fungoo to you."

At the same instant, he reached down, snatched the edge of the green baize cloth which covered the table. He jerked it towards him with venomous force, scattering cards, money, chips and their drinks over the players. He then balled the cloth in his hands and threw it into Kearns' lap before he turned away back to the door. It slammed hard behind him, so that even on his couch on the far side of the room, Sam White opened one incurious eye:

"Bad loser."

As he charged down the hall to the lifts, Steve frowned as some of Fred's words came back to him—the remarks about Brizard disappearing. He had echoed so much of what Kovakian had said to him outside the morgue. He travelled down in the lift and was still worrying away at the now-burgeoning idea as he stood irresolutely on the hotel steps. His explosion with Fred and his poker-playing companions had allowed him to let off steam and lower his internal pressure, but had brought no lasting satisfaction.

At last, he started down the steps, allowing his belligerent stare to fall upon a middle-aged lady tourist from Massachusetts who was struggling up them after a foot-sore day at the major Paris churches and museums:

"Oh, the hell with it." He was so wrapped up in his troubles that he was surprised when the lady who found herself thus addressed, gave a little scream and ran up the remainder of the steps to disappear into the sanctuary of the hotel lobby.

He kicked his way for a few yards down the street, then glanced round for a taxi. There was none in sight, so his footsteps next turned briskly towards the steps that led down to the Metro. As he went, he remembered that he still had a quantity of Bourbon stashed away in his apartment; this seemed to be his best choice of company for the night—comforting and unable to answer back until the morning.

Across the road from the entrance to the Hotel Raphael, the occupants of the black Citroen watched him slip into the gaping maw of the Metro, then the driver started the engine and it slipped out into traffic. They had assumed that he would wait for a cab and were caught unawares and unable to follow him.

Kurt, who was driving, took the car to the street that passed by the entrance to the short cul-de-sac that led into Steve's apartment block. The men were relieved when he emerged from the Metro steps at the end of the street and walked briskly to the turning without glancing round at them. Kurt was all for making a move that night, but Wilson and Fortuit counselled them to wait until the morning.

Steve regained the quiet sanity of his apartment in peace. He went from room to room, collecting all the opened and full bottles of liquor that he had. They came to a respectable number; he would certainly not go short of a drink that night.

He settled himself in to a bout of heavy drinking, all the time his mind churning over the idea that Kovakian had put into it. He was rapidly coming to the conclusion that anything would be better than the dead end that Brizard had now placed him in. He had no agents now operating in the field in France, only Kovakian's unofficial activities to add to his own—and he was supposed to stay tied to his desk. With these and similar thoughts backed up with liberal quantities of Bourbon, Steve's mood was dissipated if not satisfied.

By the time he staggered to his bed, determined not to spend another night sleeping himself into stiffness in a chair, he was determined that he would be out of his office in Paris and on Brizard's trail himself, no matter what Fred Williams might have to say on the subject.

Outside, as he slept, it was Kurt who remained on duty in the parked black Citroen, to be relieved by Fortuit in the early hours. They were mindful of their charge to get Steve Ventura before they returned to Marseilles and had decided that the next day would provide the best opportunity. The streets would be particularly busy on a Friday, and Calmet had trained them to be specialists on attack in a crowd situation. They fully expected to be able to report Steve Ventura's elimination to their masters before the day was out.

CHAPTER THREE

Another night of drinking had left Steve mentally and physically well below par. He had woken late, his head splitting, his mouth filled with an acrid, poisonous taste. He had showered and got through two pots of black coffee before he felt in good enough condition to contemplate facing the outside world.

It was Friday and Fridays meant policy meetings at the Embassy. Thanks to his activities on Thursday, Fred Williams, who presided, never let them start much before noon, so Steve could still be at his desk in good time.

His memory of his meeting with Fred and his interruption of the poker school the night before came back to him jigsaw-fashion as he dressed and, by the time he was ready to leave the apartment, he knew that he didn't want to attend the meeting. Mentally crossing his fingers, he called in to see if he could give it a miss.

When he had got past an indignant Janet, who, in spite of her lack of humour, had worked out the other two words in Steve's message, Fred's voice sounded cautious:

"Hello, Steve. You O.K.?"

Steve cleared his throat:

"Sure thing, Fred. Listen, can I skip the meeting today. I've got a lot on over Frank."

Fred gave an audible sigh of relief. Obviously it was

a confrontation that he had not been looking forward to either:

"Sure thing. You do what you have to. Why don't you take a few days R & R. You deserve it."

Steve had thanked him and hung up, immediately dialling Rita's number. It was engaged. He waited a few minutes and tried again. This time there was no reply. He would just have to try again later.

Still hung over and wrapped in his own thoughts, he left the apartment and walked down the cul-de-sac to the main road. If he had been in shape, he would have seen the black Citroen parked on the corner, the driver sitting at the wheel. As he crossed to buy a paper off the old street seller who spent the day on the opposite corner to the cafe, he would have noticed the man standing beside the battered kiosk, or the other man, leaning against the wall outside the cafe, who, seeing him cross, folded his own paper and began to cross after him.

But Steve saw none of these details until it was too late. He picked up a paper and handed over the money. As he turned away, the man by the kiosk moved forward, treading on his foot. At the same moment the other man rammed something hard and round into the small of his back and said quietly in his ear:

"You will get in the car, please."

Steve glanced round for any sign of a diversion that could help him, but, seeing none, he did as he had been asked. As the little party approached the door of the car, the driver jumped out and opened the back door. Steve slid in to the back seat and the man holding the gun got in beside him. He recognised them all from files of photographs he kept in his office.

Wilson was sitting next to him and, as they got in the front, Kurt was the driver, Fortuit in the passenger seat. He felt a frisson of excitement mixed with fear. This was a real link with Jacques Brizard, but it could turn out to be the last he would learn before he died.

Kurt started the car and it slid smoothly into the flow of traffic. He drove briskly towards the Seine and the Quai d'Orsay. Steve noticed that Kurt seemed to be having uncanny luck with the traffic lights.

For five minutes they drove in silence, Steve's flickering eyes taking everything in. The fear that was knotting with tension in the pit of his stomach had wiped out the hangover as if it had never existed and he was fully alert. The back doors seemed normal, no special locks, but, at the speed they were travelling and with fast-moving traffic all round them, there seemed to be no chance of escape that way—but if the car had to stop, then he would see.

His eyes flicked constantly between the three men. The two in the front were apparently taking no notice of him. As for Wilson, he sat relaxed, the gun resting on his thigh, pointed at Steve, but the man's hand slack on the butt. Steve rolled his newspaper, trying to make the action look like the result of nerves. Inside he was keying himself up for the chance of a break. Sooner or later, they would have to hit a red light. All he estimated he needed was five seconds of surprise.

The car turned smoothly into the Quai d'Orsay and approached the lights outside the Gare d'Orsay and the Metro entrance next to it. Kurt was driving one lane from the station kerb. As he approached the lights they started to change. Kurt might have made it across before the red signalled but for a middle-aged woman and a poodle who stepped directly in his path. He slammed on the brakes, a reflex action, and the Citroen tilted forward.

It was the moment for which Steve had been waiting. As Wilson lurched forward in the back seat, he hit him across the face with his newspaper, opened the door, jumped out and dashed across the front of a halting car and into the mouth of the Metro entrance.

By the time Wilson had grabbed for the door handle, the other car was blocking the exit and he and Fortuit were forced to slide out on the far side. Fortuit ordered Kurt to park the car and join them, then was stuck for a moment in the road as the traffic started up again. By the time the two pursuers reached the Metro entrance Steve was a good thirty seconds clear of them.

He took the dive across the road and down the steps in one fluid movement, feeling as if his feet were hardly touching the ground. There were a few people on the concourse leading to the ticket barriers and platforms, but not enough to hide amongst. He glanced at the indicator board which told him that the train on the lefthand platform would be the first to leave.

The nearest platform entrances were blocked by small knots of people showing their tickets and going through the barriers, so Steve sprinted further down the concourse, saw an unguarded barrier and dived underneath it, before stepping aboard the train.

He pushed his way to the end of the carriage where his position commanded a run to both a door onto the platform and the further door that gave out onto the cavernous track into which the Metro tunnels disappeared as if into some huge dark neolithic cavern. He unfolded his newspaper, put it up to shield his face and glanced the way he had come.

Steve had found sanctuary not a moment too soon. Fortuit was the first man down the steps, closely followed by a panting Wilson. They glanced down the concourse as he had done, then began to trot down, squinting across the platforms at the occupants of each train.

Fortuit let his eyes rake the carriage in which Steve was trying to hide, then abruptly he turned away as Kurt came down the concourse to join the other searchers. Steve sensed he had been spotted at the moment it occurred.

A man got on the train and stood next to him. He turned, shoved the opened paper in the man's surprised hands, then opened the far door and jumped down on to the tracks. In a moment he had put two of the enormous metal supports that held up the concourse and arch of the old Gare d'Orsay Station that stood above the Metro between himself and the train.

Fortuit, Wilson and Kurt made their way through separate barriers before running for Steve's carriage. Fortuit was first on the train, his gun held in his pocket, his free hand snatching away the newspaper. It took a second for the trick to sink in, and, in that lapse of time the train doors shut as the train prepared to move into the tunnel.

The train's slow movement changed the sightlines of the fleeing American's cover and Fortuit glimpsed him running across the deserted tracks. The three men forced open the off-side door and dropped down onto the tracks, drawing their guns as they began their pursuit into the labyrinth.

Fortuit was the first to spot the fleeing man and fired wildly down the tunnel at him. Steve was making the last narrow crossing to a staircase which he prayed led up to the old station above, and as the sound of the ricochet echoed round him, he jumped up on one of the huge concrete buttresses that supported the iron pillars which arched to the roof. He pressed himself against the blind side of the structure, waiting the opportunity to make the dash across the open space to the concrete stairs.

The stairs were dimly lit by one wall light and Steve

could see that the bottom was blocked with piles of old rubbish over which he could easily clamber. Halfway up the area that was visible to him, there stood some oil drums, which could provide useful cover if he made the gap. For the moment all he could do was listen to the noise made by his pursuers and pray that they had not seen him reach his sanctuary.

The first mistake that Fortuit had made was to car on the Paris streets, in the power of three men underestimate the ingenuity of one unarmed man in a with guns. Now, in his efforts to flush his quarry out, he made the second one. He sent Wilson off to the left and Kurt off to the right of the tunnel, to move down the sides, while he took the centre.

Neither Kurt nor Wilson glanced round as Steve spotted them as they entered his line of vision. He could only hold his breath and wait. He was able to place Fortuit from the sound of his movements, becoming aware that the man was almost directly behind him on the other side of the pillar. The gun was the first thing that Steve saw. It poked out into his line of vision and the man holding it followed slowly. Fortuit was coming between him and the steps.

Steve braced himself and, as Fortuit was three-quarters in front of him, with his back to the fugitive, he jumped. The gunman went down, his dropped weapon clattering along the ground. Steve did not waste time on the fight, but pulled himself away and made a dash for the steps. He was climbing over the rubbish as Fortuit groped for his gun and called out to the others. A bullet smacked off the concrete wall behind his head and Kurt ran up, preparing to take a second shot. He came too close to the stair rails and one of the oil drums caught him on the side as Steve threw it over the edge. As Kurt fell, he turned and sprinted round the bend in the staircase up into the darkness.

The flight was long and steep, much longer than he had anticipated. At the top was a door with frosted glass panels. Hearing the sound of his pursuers regaining their balance and composure below him, his heart sank. He hurled himself against the door and fell over as it swung open to his weight. As he picked himself up he found that he was on the huge, dirty deserted concourse above the platforms of the old, abandoned station. He turned to see if there was anything that could hold up his pursuers further and, but for his lack of breath, he would have laughed out loud to see the key in the door through which he had just crashed.

He shut the door and locked it, then turned to survey his possible means of escape. The steps at the far end of the concourse were blocked off by locked railings, so the only way was up. On the far side, above the platforms, was the old glass wall of the terminus, surmounted by the huge, now stilled, clock. An open doorway on the other side of the platforms seemed to lead to it.

He regained his breath and ran across the huge area. Behind him he could hear his pursuers reach the top of the steps and crash against the door. They made two attempts at getting through by brute force before Fortuit used his gun-butt to smash one of the frosted glass panels and reached through to unlock it. Steve made the cover of his own doorway only seconds before the three men came out onto the concourse.

Inside, as he had hoped he was on a catwalk that ran the length of the glass wall, rendered opaque by age and grime. It was the lowest of a series of catwalks, each running the width of the wall, the ladder to the next set at the opposite end each time. With the distance to cover on each level, Steve made only slow progress upwards, but, each time he passed a crack or hole in the glass, he was happy to see that his pursuers were busy searching the side rooms for him, without a thought for the direction in which Steve was heading.

The upper-most catwalk led to an iron door. It opened at his touch and led Steve out onto the roof of the old station. From where he stood he could see across the river a spectacular view of much of the Paris that he knew and had come to admire and love during his stay in the capital. But there was little time to stop and admire now. He went across the roof and dropped down a level onto the roof of the next building. On the far side of this was an alley, an iron fire escape leading down into it. He clambered down, then walked along the alley emerging into a main road on the far side of the block to the Quai.

He hailed the first passing taxi he saw and, as Brizard's men continued to blunder through the old station, he was speeding his way towards Sureté headquarters and Inspector Briac.

When he demanded to see Briac, he was told that the policeman was not immediately available and was invited to wait at a desk that was in a large open-plan area on the first floor of the building. The desk was by a window and Steve sat on the visitor's side, twiddling his thumbs with increasing impatience as he stared out at the dull sky. Occasionally other officers passing by asked if they could be of any assistance, but he waved them away and had chewed through his whole supply of unlit cigarettes before Briac arrived and greeted him with a cheery wave and the hope that he had not kept him waiting.

Steve told the story of his kidnapping quickly, concisely and without any unnecessary elaboration—the professional report of one policeman to another. Briac sent a junior officer for a series of mug shot books and

Steve was able to pick out shots of Wilson, Kurt and Fortuit without too much difficulty.

Briac took the photographs, picked up a phone and asked for a check on the whereabouts of the three men from the Marseilles police, reading out numbers from the backs of the shots to the man who took the order. When Steve said he had time to wait, the two men talked about everything and everybody that came into their heads—except Brizard and the Matthews case. It seemed an eternity before the phone on the desk rang. Briac answered it, listened for a moment, then:

"It is not possible? All three?"

He replaced the receiver and rose:

"I'm afraid you will have to excuse me, I will be back in a moment."

He scooped up the three pictues and took them with him. As to time, he was as good as his word and, when he returned just a few minutes later, he threw the pictures back to Steve's side of the desk. He was frowning:

"Are you absolutely certain that it was these three men who attacked you this morning?"

Steve grunted:

"Quite sure. I never forget a face—especially if it belongs to someone who is trying to kill me."

Briac was silent, sucking his teeth for a moment as he thought, then:

"Steve, I have just spoken to Marseilles. None of these men could possibly have attacked you, because they are not in Paris. As a matter of fact, none of them has left Marseilles for the past two months."

Steve sighed, with muscle like Brizard, what other answer could he have expected from Marseilles. A man who wielded as much national political influence, would have no difficulty squaring away a little thing like an attempted killing with the police authorities. He stood up wearily:

"Well, I guess I must have made a mistake. I'm sorry to have wasted your time."

Briac glanced round as he waved him down, his expression signifying that they were in too public a place for him to talk freely. He said, almost in an undertone:

"Obviously they have not left Marseilles. They work for Brizard."

Steve pricked up his ears. This was the first overt sign that Briac was not just neutral in his fight with Jacques Brizard. At last, he said heavily:

"Tell me, if you were me, what would you do if someone was trying to kill you?"

"Are you asking me as a man—or as a policeman?"

"Why—is there a difference?"

Briac smiled widely:

"Oh, my impatient friend, you are naive. Of course there is a difference, the biggest in the world. As a private man I might kill in passion or in anger, but as a policeman I am paid to keep my emotions under tight control."

"Well," shrugged Steve. "They don't pay me that much."

Briac held up his hand as he glanced round again:

"Wait. I can understand your frustration and anger. But that is the worst time for a man to make a move as a man. Four years ago a colleague of mine was moved to a similar gesture of impatience."

"What happened?"

Briac shrugged:

"I had to attend his execution. I even remember a man who hired a professional killer to do his job of killing for him. I had to attend his execution too."

Outwardly, Steve gave no sign of special interest in the turn the conversation was taking, but inwardly his mind computed Briac's possible motives for turning his thoughts into such channels. He eventually considered that there would be no harm in playing Briac's remarks by ear:

"Whose execution, the killer?"

Briac clapped his hands with pleasure as he laughed:

"I said you were naive and innocent. No, of course not the killer. The man who hired him."

Steve was silent and Briac glanced quickly round the room before rising and saying quietly:

"Come with me. We will go to my office. We will forget all this morbid talk of killer and executions and speak of more pleasant things for a while."

Steve rose and shook his head:

"No, I have no time. I have places to get to. I've wasted the whole morning already."

Briac placed himself squarely in front of the American so that Steve could see the anxious look on his face. At the same time, his voice was light:

"But my friend, I must insist. What would happen if those three men, who of course have never left Marseilles, are waiting for the opportunity of another chance to kill you—then we might never have time for our little chat."

Steve allowed himself to be led up a flight of stairs and along a corridor of blank doors to Briac's own office. He could feel a rising excitement, as if a piece of a complicated jigsaw was falling into place that would allow the whole of the rest of the puzzle to be solved.

The room was a comfortable cubicle, no bigger than his own at the Embassy. All policemen are forced to exist in small corners until they are needed, he thought, though it is usually too late when anyone finds them.

There were comfortable chairs on each side of the desk and Briac waved him into one, before going to the corner behind the desk where there stood an open wine crate. He pulled out a bottle, taking from a desk drawer two glasses and a corkscrew:

"Would you like some wine."

Steve felt impatient but realised that there was nothing to be gained and much to be lost in rushing the man. He shrugged:

"I can take it or leave it."

Briac drew the cork with loving care, filled both glasses and handed one to Steve:

"I am sorry, it should be allowed to breathe, but we do not have time for all the niceties. It is Chateau Iquem. A friend of mine sent a case to me. You should learn about such things while you are in my country—have you ever tasted it before?"

Steve held the glass up to the light:

"I don't think so."

Briac produced another bottle from the crate:

"Take this bottle. You should enjoy it at your leisure. It really is a very good wine."

Impatience made Steve accept the bottle with singular bad grace that would have put off a less consciously charming man than the Inspector:

"Thanks very much—but all wines taste like Muscatel to me."

"Muscatel?"

Steve felt more relaxed on discovering that there was at any rate one thing Briac didn't know about:

"It's a wine I used to drink when I was a kid in Jersey. The people next door used to take in a lot of it and the other kids in the neighbourhood used to steal it for a dare. There wasn't much else to do—all the hub caps had been stolen years before."

Briac laughed dutifully and raised his glass:

"To your success."

"Success?"

"Why, yes," smiled Briac, leaning forward confidentially. "To me as a policeman, Jacques Brizard is a respectable upright citizen. Now, if you were really able to prove otherwise. . . ." He left the sentence unfinished and leant back in his chair without taking his eyes off the other man.

After a pause, Steve said:

"What was his name?"

"The man who gave me the wine?", grinned Briac.

"No," snapped Steve with growing impatience. "The killer."

The policeman's eyes widened with well-feigned amazement. He drained his glass at one gulp and put it down on the desk with a bang:

"You're not serious?"

"How much would it cost?"

Briac leant forward. He seemed to be choosing his words with the greatest care before uttering them, as if he wanted to be quite sure that they would not be open to any misinterpretation at some unspecified later date:

"Do I understand aright—are you asking me to co-operate in a scheme for premeditated murder?"

Now it was Steve's turn to choose his words with the greatest care. He felt that he was walking into a mine-field, where every step counted:

"I'm not asking you to compromise yourself in any way. I just want you to tell me how much you think his service might cost—assuming that you knew such a man."

Briac shrugged:

"I would have very little idea. I cannot draw on any large expense account. I cannot even authorise funds to pay for little details like false Canadian passports."

"But I can."

The eyes of the two men locked on to one another, each one debating inwardly just how far it was possible to trust the other. It was Briac whose eyes dropped first. He sat back in his chair, his fingertips together. After an infinity of waiting, Steve relaxed as he pronounced:

"There just might be such a man—and he might be available for hire at this time. But the killing of a man like Jacques Brizard only offers fifty-fifty odds of success and subsequent safety."

"I'm sure the odds would be short. Marcus and Matthews are proof of that."

Briac nodded:

"But for the right price, well, I suppose a professional such as the man I have just referred to might be prepared to consider the risks."

Steve was openly excited now:

"Who do you have in mind?"

Briac rose, smiling his most irritating smile:

"Come now, Mr. Ventura, what would make you think I had any such specific person in mind. I was merely—how do you put it—speculating. I didn't realise that you were taking me that seriously."

Steve erupted:

"Well, what the hell has all this been about? Why did you bring me to your Goddam office and chat away about professional killers and secret funds. It may be a laugh to you, but I've had two top operatives wasted in the past six months—and all on one lousy assignment, putting the goods on Jacques Brizard. If we could do that perhaps then there'd be a chance for millions of people to lead normal lives, for the thousands of kids who die each year from dangerous drugs to live—and to you all this is the subject for some amusing theoretical speculation—."

Steve broke off as Briac, who had maintained his smile throughout the other man's tirade, winked and held up a hand for silence. He walked over to the door, opened it suddenly, glanced down the corridor, closed it and walked back to his chair, clapping his hands together as if to signify that he was now prepared to get down to business. During this pantomime, the reasons for caution had dawned on Steve and the anger had ebbed out of him:

"Just like the man I have in mind, Mr. Ventura, I am a very cautious man where such matters are concerned."

As he spoke, he refilled his glass and checked Steve's untouched drink. He handed Steve's glass to him once more, clinked glasses, then sipped his own afresh:

"Yes, as I say, he is a cautious man. That's one of the things that makes him such a good man. We know, of course, of several killings in which he has been involved, but we have never been able to prove anything, to get enough even to justify questioning him."

"What else do you know about him?"

"Well, when he works, which isn't often, he gets paid top money. He lives well, though, spends it quickly when he has it. He has many women, but none permanent. He lives alone—oh, and he especially enjoys driving fast cars."

Steve took a deep breath. This was the sixty four thousand dollar question:

"I'd like a meeting with him. Can it be arranged?"

"No problem," beamed the Frenchman. "Quite unofficially, you understand?"

Steve relaxed enough to smile at this sally and sipped his wine as he replied:

"Of course."

"How does it taste?"

He grinned:

"Like Muscatel—I'm sorry."

Briac swallowed but shrugged off the criticism of French wine, a subject on which he was fanatical:

"Well, if everything was to the same standard and taste for everyone, it would be a dull world. Come, I will arrange for a police car to take you to the Embassy."

Steve shook his head:

"No thanks, I'll be okay on my own."

Briac frowned, seemingly genuinely distressed:

"But those men. They may try again."

Steve shrugged:

"I'll take my chances on that. What I can't face is the questions I'll be asked if I turn up at the Embassy in a French police car."

Briac smiled and bowed his visitor out of the room. Steve's logic was impeccable.

Steve Ventura lay in bed that night, wrestling with the urgent desire for a cigarette and running the conversation with Briac through the inner camera of his mind, over and over again, looking for any unexpected angles or motives the Frenchman might have in coming into the open with such an offer.

All the rest of the day as he went through routine chores and reports in his office he had waited anxiously for the detective to call. His only trauma had occurred when he had signed the recommendation forms regarding the pension to be paid by the Government to Rita Matthews, a puny sum as an exchange for her husband's life.

He had realised that for two days he had not spoken to her and, when all the form-filling and dictation was done, he put in a call, but once again there was no reply. It did not sadden him as much as it had previously, he was too stimulated by the prospect that he might have found a new way of dealing with the problem of Jacques Brizard.

At six o'clock, his nerve had given way and he had called the Sureté, only to be told that Inspector Briac was not in the building and no one had a note of his whereabouts. Steve had to be content just to wait.

He had gone over to the Raphael Bar, hoping that the policeman might be there and had ended up having a couple of social drinks with Embassy colleagues, all of whom wanted to talk about Matthews' death and to commiserate with him. He had not been able to stand it for long and had made his excuses early, hailing the second cab that came along as a matter of caution and spending the journey back to his apartment glancing out of the back window to make sure that he was not being followed.

As for the apartment itself, he entered it cautiously, but was relieved to find that nothing seemed to have been touched—the apartment had not been entered.

For dinner he made a plate of scrambled eggs and washed them down with a couple of beers. Afterwards he had tried once more to call the policeman, but Briac was still unavailable.

He prepared for bed and sat up waiting for the call, running the conversation over in his mind again and again. At last, he slipped off into a much-needed sleep.

He woke with a start to the pealing of the phone. The light was still on from the time he had drifted into sleep and the clock at his bedside registered just past three in the morning. He picked up the receiver:

"Yes?"

He was relieved to hear Briac's voice:

"Steve?"

"Yes, Briac."

"I have arranged a meeting."

Steve wanted to give a whoop of excitement but contented himself with snapping out:

"When?"

"Tomorrow afternoon, three o'clock. In the park. The bench near the children's amusement area, on the hill—you know where I mean?"

"Yes. Thanks. How will I know him?"

Briac laughed:

"I almost forgot. You are to carry a large white handkerchief and you will blow your nose with alarming frequency, as if you have a bad cold. The other man will be similarly equipped, by way of a recognition reply."

Steve wanted to thank Briac for the work he had put in, but the policeman broke the connection at once. Steve got out of bed and padded to the kitchen to get a cold beer. He knew that the news he had just received would make sleep impossible for a while. His mind raced over the details. He had checked with his files that day and knew that he would have no trouble drawing on the secret fund at short notice—for that he would be answerable to no one—not even Fred Williams. At the same time, with his seniority at the Embassy he was immune to awkward questions later if anything misfired and would be spirited back home—albeit in probably permanent disgrace—if anything went wrong.

The more he thought about it, the more he became convinced that this was the only reasonable way of dealing with Brizard. He marvelled that he had not come to that conclusion on his own a long time ago. He supposed it to be his damned conscience. All his life he had worked within a framework of the law, within rules he respected, in a manner that he had been trained for and approved of.

It had always been good enough up until now—

finding the proof of wrong-doing and letting the courts take over from then—but increasingly in recent years the courts had seemed to be a way in which the malefactors could tie up any action against them before slipping through the web of deceit and confusion to freedom, acquitted and unrepentant.

This time, too, it was very important that something be done about the whole drugs situation, especially the French connection with the international marketing of these lethal products. The big men exerted huge local political and protective influence. They could not be touched, no matter what angle the problem was approached from.

If an informer went to the police, somewhere amongst them would be a man who would report back and the informer would disappear or be killed before any action could be taken. If the informer was well-enough protected to tell his story to an investigating magistrate, these men would, as like as not, be in the debt of one of the powerful political machines—phone calls would be made and the case would disappear into an investigative limbo. It was a dream set-up for the men in this dangerous trade—reminiscent of Chicago in the twenties and thirties—and a nightmare for the international police groups who were trying to stamp out the drug traffic.

No, thought Steve, this is the only way. Find a loner, a man without any connections on either side of the law. To the professional assassin this would be a job like any other—riskier than some, probably easier than others, for there is always a glaring chink in the armour of a man who bases his whole way of life on protection.

Steve finished the beer and got back into bed. He must try to sleep, for tomorrow was to be an exciting and fulfilling day for him.

CHAPTER FOUR

Steve arrived at the entrance to the park a good fifteen minutes ahead of the time for his appointment.

He had slept in until very nearly ten o'clock and had awakened refreshed and ready for the excitement of the day, unaccompanied by the hangover and feeling of depression that had been his constant companion since the night of Frank Matthews' death.

As he showered, shaved and dressed, he amused himself by imagining the physical appearance and mental attitude of the loner he was going to meet—a man who would squeeze the trigger and kill a fellow human being without any mercy or inquisitiveness, merely because he had a job to do and was being paid to kill. He didn't have much success duplicating the attitude of mind of such a man and he finally dismissed the speculation from his mind and concentrated on making himself a hearty breakfast. With hope for a solution in the affair of Jacques Brizard, his appetite had returned.

After breakfast, he called Sally at the Embassy and

told her that he would be in sometime after three. He told her to speak to no one else about his absence, but to have the special file on the secret fund ready for when he came in. The girl was obviously bursting with questions, but he cut her short and replaced the receiver.

Outside, the day was blustery, the dark clouds heavy with autumn rain. He slipped on his raincoat and slipped his U.S. Government issue pistol from its hiding place—in a plastic bag in the freezer compartment of the fridge—and slipped it into his raincoat pocket. After the events of the day before, he was determined to be as cautious as possible.

He followed this same rule when he reached the entrance to the block—hanging back in the shadows within the doorway and surveying the street carefully before venturing forth. He was on the alert from his first glance. The cul-de-sac itself was empty, but a man was lounging against the wall by the news kiosk, reading a paper.

Steve watched him for a while but he did not glance down the street so, eventually, he decided to brazen it out. With one hand clutched round the butt of the gun hidden in his pocket, Steve started forward down the cul-de-sac. He walked slowly, but the man did not appear to look up.

The moment of greatest danger would be as he went past, and he found the tension building as he approached the man. He was only five paces away when the stranger folded his paper, lifted a hand and said:

"Monsieur Ventura. Inspector Briac's compliments. I will not be following you, I am placed here to protect your apartment."

He was taken aback at Steve's broad smile:

"Thank the Inspector for me."

His hand slid away from the gun butt and he walked down the street with a brisker tread. At least his instincts about the man had been right—he was a watcher. But it was a relief to find that your own side was in the field as well as the enemy. Still, it showed Steve that his nerves were becoming over-stretched. He would have to calm down a bit, the Brizard business was getting on top of him. If he went on reacting like this to the slightest detail, he could find himself back in Washington with a desk job in some ignored corner—or even pensioned off.

If these sort of nerves were the result of a year at a desk in the Embassy, then the sooner he was back in the field the better—if, he thought wryly, they would ever have him back, bearing in mind the plan he was hoping to put under way this afternoon.

As he entered the park gates and walked with measured strides towards the children's play area, his step was lighter and his manner more relaxed than they had been for many days. He glanced at his watch. It was far too early, there was still plenty of time.

Steve walked over to watch the children at play and was irresistibly reminded, to his regret, of Kevin Matthews and his mother, Rita. Many of the children were riding a slow roundabout, each child carrying a short wooden stick. As the roundabout wheeled round, they were faced with small gingerbread men, hanging from a post that leant over to them. In each man was a hole and, by getting the stick through the hole, the children were able to capture a piece of the gingerbread for themselves. As they were captured or knocked to the ground, a girl was adding new men to the pole.

Steve watched the antics with some amusement, noting that it was the little girls who seemed to be better at this appointed task—and wryly noting that this was a lesson they would learn for later life, especially in the new age of equality and equal opportunity—perhaps a more up to date equivalent of 'softly, softly, catchee monkey'.

It was still only five to three but Steve, impatient for his rendezvous, walked on and down the slope of the path to the bench which was empty. He sat down and unrolled a newspaper, pulling the handkerchief out of his pocket at the same time and making a great pantomime of blowing his nose as he glanced round at the almost-deserted area. For a minute or two his only visible companions were two women and an assortment of children.

Then, from the bottom of the path, a thin man came up the slope, walking briskly, a briefcase clutched in one hand, his overcoat buttoned against the chill—holding a white handkerchief in his free hand. The man paused to blow his nose at elaborate length, before walking briskly on in Steve's direction.

Steve reciprocated in kind and this pantomime was followed by another nose-blow from the newcomer. The American tensed himself, waiting for the man to come over. To his surprise, the man did not even seem to notice him and instead, went briskly on up the slope, pausing at the top to give himself another few moments of loud nose-blowing.

Steve almost laughed out loud at the ridiculous charade he had just gone through and all for the benefit of some poor Frenchman with a cold.

At three-fifteen, Steve was becoming angry and depressed again at the thought that his contact was not going to show up. He had not glanced again towards the sounds of the voices of the laughing children in their play area or he would have noticed the quietly-dressed man watching him from the other side of the round-about.

Steve rose stiffly, filled with disappointment. He was

just about to move off, find a phone and call Briac to ask what had happened when a hand came down on his shoulder, causing him to jump almost out of his skin and a voice said:

"Good God, Steve, fancy seeing you."

He whirled round, stuffing the white handkerchief guiltily into his pocket. A moment of non-recognition, then:

"Good God, Johnny Deray."

He was much as Steve always remembered him. Tall, blond with a laughing mouth but cold grey-blue eyes; the slightest hint of fat, but nothing to say that he was as yet out of condition. He remembered all this from their years in Africa in a flash of delighted memory that took almost no time at all. As he thought back it seemed to him that while Johnny had not changed, their time in Africa was spent on another planet in a different age, not just a few short years before. They shook hands warmly and Johnny asked:

"How are you, you old son of a bitch."

His English was perfect—had always been, Steve recalled.

For almost a year in those far off days of the Congo crisis and the short-lived Republic of Katanga, Johnny Deray had been Steve Ventura's other half. They had eaten, slept and fought together, each man protecting the other's back.

It had been after the Belgians had given independence to their African colonies and the great powers had rushed in to try and get the most they could in the way of political and economic control of the new country, taking advantage of the vacuum that followed Belgian withdrawal.

Steve had been operating within the CIA at that time and he had been sent out to Katanga on a reconnaissance and liaison mission with the gendarmerie, after Tshombe had made his brave stand against the central government and had opted for independence for his state.

Johnny Deray was living locally. With a Belgian father and an English mother, he had spent most of his life in Central Africa and was an expert in the terrain and the labyrinthine politics of the area. He also realised that if he just stood aside and let the various independent factions in the country rend themselves apart, there would no longer be room for him and his kind in the area.

He had volunteered as a mercenary, working as an interpreter and then as a member of the mercenary groups that Tshombe had hired in from White South Africa and the disaffected ex-professionals of Europe. At the same time, the CIA had singled him out and recruited him to work for them in the area. When things hotted up, Steve had been sent in to liaise and advise.

It had never failed to surprise him, when the crunch came and the mercenaries took to the bush to fight off the Congolese army and the mixed units put in to quell the country by the U.N. Security Council, that Johnny, on the surface so good-humoured, easy-going and gentle, should turn into such a ruthless killer in defence not only of himself, but of Steve.

The crunch had finally come with the imminent collapse of Tshombe's administration. The CIA had radioed Steve to abort and somehow get across the border into Angola where the military and the CIA were cooperating to spirit him away as if an American agent had never been in the area. This was the moment when Johnny would have been expected to stay put with the other mercenaries and fight it out, at least to defend what he believed in.

But when Steve told him of his orders, Johnny was

only too happy to come along. He explained that he thought Katanga was already doomed, and anyway was no place for such men as he—and the two men had gone across country, avoiding the patrols of both sides in order to get to safety and the airlift out.

On two occasions during their nightmare trek through the bush, Johnny had been instrumental in keeping Steve alive—and had expected no thanks or praise. It was part of his duty, and he accepted it as such.

The two men had not seen each other since Steve had been flown back to the States.

Aloud, while these thoughts were flying through his head, he laughed and shouted:

"Johnny—Jeez it's great to see you. How long's it been? Five years? Six?"

Johnny smiled his lop-sided boyish smile. He was in his middle thirties but looked ten years younger:

"Nearer nine."

Steve glanced round, looking for his appointment to still show up but there was no one else in sight:

"God, how time flies. What are you doing now?"

Johnny shrugged:

"Little bit of this, little bit of that. I've been moving around quite a bit these last few years—what about yourself?"

Steve shrugged off the question:

"Just the same old grind for the government, but official now. I'm with the Embassy. Look, Johnny, I'm supposed to have an appointment. I have to meet someone—tell you what, we could have dinner tonight. I'll just write down my number."

He scrabbled in his pocket for his pen and note pad. Johnny clapped his hands together and laughed:

"Hey, Steve, slow down, hang on a minute."

"What?"

"I'm the appointment. I'm the man you're meeting."

Steve was dumbfounded and Johnny said softly:

"I'm the man you have an appointment with."

His bewilderment showed in his features and immediately the plan he had formulated assumed totally different dimensions. This was no faceless assassin, this was an old friend. Killing Jacques Brizard was ceasing to be an objective enterprise and was about to turn into something alarmingly personal. Steve found he was suddenly genuinely frightened by the prospect. He bleated:

"What the hell are you talking about, Johnny?"

"The Contact, Steve. Don't look so surprised. It's me."

Steve could not help it—a mixture of shock and disgust that his old friend should be engaged in so brutalised an occupation as that of an assassin spread over his face. Johnny, however, seemed genuinely amused by his discomfiture:

"Listen, what are you so upset about? The money's good, the hours are short and like the fellow said when he was asked why he never touched women and children, we only kill each other."

Steve frowned, peering hard at Johnny as if that would pierce the outer shell he remembered and show him the new man beneath:

"Well, you have changed."

Johnny's smile faded into sadness. He shook his head slowly and his voice was more serious:

"No, Steve, I haven't changed. The world has. I've only changed my job. Look, I don't have a great deal of time to stand around and talk about old times. If you want someone killed just cough up my price and I'll take care of the rest."

Steve shook his head:

"No, Johnny, I can't set up a thing like this myself,

not with you. It's too personal. I'll have Briac make a deal with you."

The other man stiffened his eyes darting to left and right:

"No deal—I don't trust cops."

"I'm a cop."

"You're my friend. I can trust you, Steve. That's what friends are for—now why don't you relax and trust me."

Steve lumbered over to the bench and sat down heavily, shaking his head to clear the confusion out of it as if it was something physical that had overtaken him. At last, he said:

"What is your price. Briac was vague."

Johnny laughed:

"He would be. He can't even prove I do the jobs. That's why I'm still around. It's twenty-five thousand dollars a man—of course, if I have to act in self-defense on the way, that's a free bonus."

"Okay, I can get you twenty-five thousand."

There was a silence and Johnny was forced to break it:

"Of course, Steve, it would be a lot of help to know who and where."

Steve pulled himself together and stood up:

"The target lives in Marseilles."

"Good," nodded Johnny. "I was just thinking of taking a few days in the south. The weather here's shocking. And the who?"

"The man's name is Brizard."

"Jacques Brizard?" Johnny's face and voice were suddenly grim, he was more on the alert. Steve noticed it and thought that the other man was going to turn the job down. He was surprised to realise that, for Johnny's sake, he felt almost pleased at this apparent turn of events. He coughed:

"Yes, Jacques Brizard himself. You have second thoughts. You want to walk away from this one?"

The tension drained out of Johnny Deray's face as quickly as it had tightened it and he replaced it with the charming lop-sided smile that Steve remembered so well and which always meant trouble for someone—usually an enemy of Johnny:

"Oh, no, Steve, there's never been a job thought of that I'd turn down. It's just that Jacques Brizard is somewhat of a special and that will make it fifty thousand dollars—payable in advance."

The two men's eyes were locked on one another. Steve shivered inwardly as he saw the harsh blue of Johnny's, cold and with no compassion in them. He jerked his eyes to the ground. He knew now, after that look, that Johnny was the best man he could have found for the job. He muttered:

"Okay, Johnny, meet me here at five o'clock and I'll have the money and everything that's on file about Brizard for you."

"Okay." With a curt nod, Johnny turned on his heel and began to walk down the slope to the park exit. Steve was jerked into sudden life and called after him:

"Johnny, what happened. You can tell me."

Johnny walked back to him, his smile cool, his eyes expressionless:

"Happened, Steve?"

Steve was confused and embarrassed:

"I mean—what happened to turn you—you into—." He ended on a note of helpless embarrassment.

Johnny was sardonically amused by the older man's confusion:

"Into a killer, you mean?"

Steve could only blush and Johnny patted his arm in a reassuring gesture:

"Don't lose all your faith in human nature, Mate. Nothing happened. I'm the same man."

"Nothing?"

"Look, I'm still the same person, aren't I? I like girls—I like television, I still go and visit my mother and listen to her telling me that the younger generation is not like hers—I complain about traffic jams, just like anyone else—the terrible French telephone system—the weather—oh, I'm still the same."

As he spoke, he walked backwards, keeping Steve mesmerised with his smile. At the end of the sentence, he waved, swung round and walked briskly away.

Steve watched him until he was out of sight. His mind only got back into gear when his old friend had disappeared from view. Then, recovering himself, but with his mind still in a confusion of loyalties and beliefs, he turned and walked briskly in the opposite direction, comforting himself with the not altogether convincing thought that if Inspector Briac thought Johnny was the man for the job, then Johnny must be the best. After all, Briac would have no way of knowing of their previous friendship and work together in the Congo.

He shrugged the thoughts to the back of his mind as he passed the children's play area, but the sight of the happy, innocent faces intent on their pleasure afforded him no release from his worries. There was something inequitable about the way the world ran if plotting and murder were the instruments that had to be used to keep such faces innocent and happy.

Still, that thought brought Brizard back into his mind. If one bastard deserved to be killed, it was the drug pusher, sitting in the middle of his international web, protected against any legal sanction. Perhaps, thought Steve, Johnny might report back how he had done it, the look on Brizard's face if the killing could be done close enough. But it was a wild thought. Johnny was now a professional killer and Steve merely a client. They would never meet again, neither man would ever feel safe. This brought renewed anger against Brizard, who was to cost him three friendships instead of the two who had been his official agents.

By the time the cab he had hailed at the park entrance arrived at the Embassy, Steve Ventura had managed to compromise his fears by rationalising the justice of Brizard's death being accomplished by a personal friend rather than a faceless assassin. It was with a lighter stride that he entered the office he hated so much and told Sally to give him the file and forms so that he could draw cash on the secret fund at once.

If Sally was worried at his sudden change of mood she gave no sign of it beyond overt glances as they worked and she managed to hold back her curiosity, though at what cost to her instinctive femininity, it would be impossible to estimate.

At five o'clock Steve Ventura found himself walking past the now-deserted children's playground in a blustery wind, a small briefcase in one hand, fifty thousand dollars burning a hole in a tight linen envelope in his inside pocket. The briefcase contained all the information—and a good amount of speculation, but marked accordingly—that Steve had ever been able to amass on Jacques Brizard.

He was pleased to see that Johnny had preceded him, was now sitting on the bench waiting for him. He rose as Steve approached and smiled:

"That's a relief. There was a moment when I thought you'd change your mind and wouldn't be back. Is it on?"

Steve didn't answer him directly. Instead, he handed him the briefcase:

"All the information I could dig up on Brizard and his people."

Johnny took the briefcase and put it on the bench: "Thanks."

Steve ploughed on:

"I've done one or two other things. You'll find three different national passports, one French, in the name of John Davos. Also, in the back of the French one, you'll find a phone number. Try not to call it unless you have to—if you do, you know I'll do anything you say."

Johnny shook his head:

"Don't worry. I won't call. That's part of the rules. You're paying to be protected. Brizard's death will tell you all you have to know."

There was an awkward pause between the two men. Steve tried to break through the barrier that was between them by holding out his hand:

"Good luck, Johnny."

Johnny shook his head:

"If I depended on luck, then I'd have been out of business a long time ago."

Steve had the grace to look ashamed and confused in equal measure, so Johnny laughed to show he had been teasing and shook his hand warmly. Steve turned away, but stopped short, when Johnny called:

"Oh, Steve?"

"Yes?"

"What about the money."

Steve was frozen for a moment, then he burst out with a roar of genuine laughter, which completely broke the tension he had been feeling.

"God, Johnny. I'm sorry. I completely forgot."

He pulled out the envelope from his inside pocket and handed it to Johnny who pushed it into the pocket of his coat before picking up the briefcase and preparing to move away: Steve was more than surprised this time:

"Don't you want to count it?"

Johnny shook his head and there was no longer a smile on his face:

"I trust you, Steve."

Then he turned and walked into the dusk. Steve heaved a huge sigh as he watched him go. The wheels had been set in motion now. It was so much easier to oil and start a machine than it was to stop it. He could only pray that Johnny would be successful. He turned away bent on a mission of his own. For the first time that day, he really needed a drink.

CHAPTER FIVE

There was never a moment when Jacques Brizard was unaware that he weighed heavily on the mind of Steve Ventura in Paris, as well as dozens of similar men dotted round cities all over the world. Such thoughts, however, made only small inroads of caution on the way he made his plans. Jacques Brizard was totally dedicated to power and money through his own chosen profession, and he had achieved both to a degree that astonished even himself. Now, as Steve set in motion the latest of many plans that had been made to dispose of Brizard during his career, Brizard was laying plans, legal and illegal for his further enrichment.

On the morning after Steve's meeting with Johnny Deray, his chief preoccupations were on one plan in each sector of his affairs. He was enjoying a late breakfast on the lawn of his villa overlooking the Mediterranean outside the city, and far enough away to be spoilt neither by the industrial pollution of the great port, or the spreading urban sprawl of a vital city.

He felt placid and at ease, surrounded by his loved ones. Sitting at the glass-topped table, still munching toast and sipping coffee was his daughter Lucienne, at twenty-four a sophisticated woman who knew what she wanted and, to Brizard's relief, these wants included a loyal and abiding affection for him. He had never involved her in his nefarious activities, it was enough that she knew he was a man who was constantly in danger—but also realised that the fast cars, fast men and security she enjoyed, as she picked her selfish way through life, were the result of his labours. He was proud of her, she was as intelligent as himself and he doted on her beauty, brains and faithfulness.

On the far side of the table, on a swing seat, lay the other object of his affections, Madame Apcar, his mistress. She was in her early thirties with a shape that was totally satisfying and a brain that, in its own way, was totally satisfying to him as well. Madame Apcar never had a thought in her own head except for her appearance, her stomach and Brizard's money. These three things kept her loyal, loving and totally submissive. At the moment she was leafing idly through some fashion magazine, just looking at the pictures to decide what she liked. Reading them gave her a headache.

Behind them on the terrace, stood Wilson—there was always one bodyguard in attendance wherever Brizard went—and past him there now stepped Brizard's chef, the highest paid gastronomic entertainer in the whole of France, as Brizard was never slow to point out to the admiring guests who attended his dinner parties. He was carrying a written menu and he stood beside Brizard's chair and bowed:

"I have the special menu you asked me to prepare for the charity dinner at the Club on the eighteenth."

Brizard's dark glasses registered nothing, but his thin mouth smiled in anticipation:

"Read it—Lucienne listen to this."

The chef glanced down his handiwork to make sure that there was nothing he had forgotten:

"Well, Sir, I have suggested that we begin with the Avalanche de Hors d'Oevres, followed by the Loup de Mediterrane Flambe a la fin Champagne, with a Gewurztraminer 70, then Noisette de Chevreuil Grand Veneur and for wine a Vosne Romane 64, Salade de Mache au Mimosa, and for the dessert, I would recommend a Souffle Arlequin with Champagne Dom Perignon. Do you think that will be quite satisfactory, Monsieur?"

Brizard slipped off his dark glasses, took the menu from the man's hand, studied it for a moment, then glanced at Lucienne's face. She too seemed pleased and he handed the menu back to the chef with a nod:

"Thank you, that is perfect."

The chef bowed, turned and walked back towards the terrace. Brizard half-turned in his chair to watch him go, then turned back and said to Lucienne:

"The dinner is for charity. Do you think that our chef's Souffle Arlequin will make them open their pocketbooks." His voice was that of the educated man he was. No cheap crook had Brizard ever been, that was what had made him so powerful and so dangerous.

He watched his daughter closely from behind the glasses. Her beauty and the subtle movemnts of her body never failed to enchant and delight him. They reminded him of his long-dead wife, the one spot of sentimentality in the man's make-up. Lucienne laughed:

"I think it would take a hand grenade to open the locks that some of them keep on their pocket books, Father."

Brizard smiled with delight then turned towards his mistress:

"And what do you think, my darling?"

Madame Apcar looked up vaguely and let the magazines fall on the grass as the seat swung:

"Pardon."

Brizard smiled indulgently. She was his little weakness and he revelled in her simple stupidity:

"You should have been listening my love. This is important. It is about food."

"Ah, I will just have a green salad. I am on a diet."

Both her companions laughed this time. Brizard went on:

"No, it isn't your lunch we're talking about. We are discussing what to offer our guests at the charity gala on the eighteenth."

Madame Apcar, who hated to be asked difficult questions, uncharacteristically puckered her beautiful brow, then release came:

"If you like it, then I like it, ma chere."

Brizard glanced at his laughter:

"Lucienne, tell me, do you think there is any detail I have overlooked?"

She smiled back at him:

"Is there ever, Father?"

He nodded, satisfied, and rose:

"Very well Lucienne, you will work with me on the gala, and you, my dear, will help prepare the guest list. You know everyone with money on the coast." This last was addressed with no trace of malice at Madame Apcar, who smiled up at him, taking it as a great compliment to her ingenuity which he intended.

He made them both a small bow and turned to walk over to Wilson on the terrace, slowly, a rich man enjoying his ease, without an apparent care or conscience to bother him.

As he reached the terrace, Calmet, his lieutenant and the closest that Brizard came to having a friend, emerged through the open French windows, where he had been standing out of sight, waiting for his master. Brizard raised a hand in greeting:

"Ah, Calmet. Where is Kurt?"

The two men walked back into the house before Calmet answered:

"I left him in Paris. I told him to take another crack at that damned man Ventura."

They walked down the corridor to Brazard's deceptively book-lined study. He held up his hand angrily:

"No. He must be recalled. That approach has been a mistake from the start. When a man is in Ventura's position, political obstacles are, in the end, much more effective and less messy."

"But Kurt can—."

Brizard spun round and snatched off his dark glasses, a sign that he was angry and would not countenance an argument:

"Get hold of Kurt and tell him he's relieved of the assignment. Send him back here to Marseilles as fast as it can be arranged—right?"

Calmet felt the beads of sweat on the forehead of his habitually expressionless face. Though he regarded himself as Brizard's closest approach to a friend, and was his principal and most trusted lieutenant, he was aware that, if he ever crossed his master, that would be the end of him. Like all strong men, Brizard allowed an element of fear to take its place in any transaction he made with his men.

"Yes, Sir."

Brizard relaxed his face into a beaming smile:

"Good, Now we have a far more important problem to clear up. You had better go and see Lazar and make sure that he's managing to recruit enough chemists to refine 400 kilogrammes of base morphine on the night of the eighteenth. Do you think there'll be any problems? The charity gala provides a foolproof cover."

Calmet shook his head:

"With the arrangements, no—but Ventura . . . ?"

"Well?"

"Why have you changed your mind about killing the man. If he gets wind of this, that would mean big trouble. It's the biggest shipment the port has ever handled?"

Brizard sat down behind the huge, ornate desk. Behind him were the books of the library, to his left a bank of television screens from which he would see any part of the house and grounds at the flick of the controls. On his right the wall of books was a series of false spines, concealing a cocktail cabinet, a top-security safe and the second door to the study—a door that led into the rear of the villa's front entrance cloakroom and thus to the front entrance of the villa itself. He thought for a moment, then decided to let Calmet in on his thinking—his lieutenant was always inclined to extreme solutions:

"I don't want anything to interfere with the current operation. Now Ventura is good, I grant you that, but we've wasted his two operatives who got anywhere close to us. Even if he gets wind of the shipment, he will have no idea where or when, and that means he won't be able to move the local police into action—even if they make a token gesture, we will know about it—but, if he is killed then every policeman from here to France's borders will be alerted and buzzing and we might just get caught in the middle by accident. None of my pull will protect me then."

Calmet took a deep breath:

"If I may say so, I still think that you are underestimating him. How do we know what the men reported back. We've been lucky, but he could get lucky too."

Brizard nodded:

"But nothing happened when the shipment left, so he didn't know then. There's been no alert on the ship's movements anywhere across the Mediterranean, so we know he knows nothing yet. As to the operations we countered, he's been feinting in the dark. If he had known anything for sure, he would have kept his men better protected and the police would have been in on it, at least at the Paris level. I have good reason to know they knew nothing about the operation until the bodies were found. They just got lucky—too lucky for their own health."

He looked up in silence at the still worried Calmet and then said gently:

"Just forget about Ventura. I will give him to you to deal with later. Just make the arrangements with Lazar to put my mind at rest—and remember, no guns."

He swung his chair around to show that the interview was at an end and Calmet left his presence to find Fortuit and do his master's bidding. As soon as he was gone, Brizard flicked a switch on the bank of controls to check that Lucienne and Madame Apcar were still in the garden, then went to open his safe.

Calmet found Fortuit sitting in the car in which he had arrived at the villa. Calmet got in and ordered the man to drive him to Lazar's garage, the front of his real business as Brizard's chief chemist in the business of drug refining and adulteration.

Fortuit went slowly down the drive, Calmet sitting, his mind still teeming with the arguments he would have given Brizard for the elimination of Steve Ventura, if his fear had not overcome him. Still, Brizard usually knew best, he had to admit.

The car reached the gatehouse in front of the locked gates that led to the deserted coast road into Marseilles. He waited while the guard in the gatehouse came out and glanced towards the car. Calmet stared up at the TV camera that stood above the gate, its red light on, which signified that Brizard was watching him. He nodded towards the lens as the guard held his rifle in one hand and used the other to open the gates.

Outside, as the car went through and the gates closed behind it, the only cover was provided by a line of scrub that separated the road from the sea cliffs, while tall firs stood at either side of the gates. The car turned towards Marseilles and drove off at high speed.

Johnny Deray, lying in the scrub across the road, smiled to himself as he put down the binoculars. He had seen all he wanted to see. The villa seemed impregnable to anything but a commando attack and that wasn't Johnny's style. Anyway, Brizard would be bound to have bolt holes in case of trouble, and the killer knew he wouldn't have a second chance, even if he lived after the first attack.

He went back down on the beach and began to walk in the direction of his car. He was feeling very tired. Immediately after leaving Steve Ventura, he had packed his bags, checking that every item was devoid of any name tag, maker's label or laundry mark that might be used to identify him and had then climbed into his car of the moment—the latest Alfa Romeo.

By dint of concentrated driving he had arrived in the Marseilles area, thanks to the new super-highway, just before dawn and, before finding a bolt hole in the town, he had decided to case the villa. He was pleased with what he had seen. At least he wouldn't waste any time on secretive night operations. There was another way to get into the villa and this was the next thing to concentrate on. The key to his entry would be Lucienne—but in order to make any headway with her, the first thing on the agenda would be a few hours sleep. She was bound to come into the city at some point during the day and it was Johnny's experience that with such rich, pampered females, the time they got bored was somewhere round noon. He reckoned he would have time to find a place in the city, take an hour's rest and be back in time to make his own special kind of contact. If he missed her, he had all the time in the world. You had to go slowly with a risky operation like this. There was always tomorrow.

He drove quickly into Marseilles and made straight for the waterfront, near the docks, but also near a Marina for those who used the sea for more leisurely pursuits. He parked outside a modest looking pensione, went in, registered for a room, handing in an English passport in the name of Davos.

The room was small and quiet and he settled on the bed to study the file that Steve had given him. The picture the American agent had might not be complete but Johnny would have to know and remember every little fact he could strain out of it if he was to have a chance of remaining alive.

Fortuit drove Calmet to the outskirts of Marseilles where stood the garage which Lazar used as his front. He drove round the side of the building and straight into the yard of the mechanic's workshop at the rear. Lazar was tinkering with one car, but Fortuit and Calmet noticed a stranger—a fat mechanic with a large moustache, who was working on the engine of another car.

Calmet got out and went over to Lazar who wiped his hands on an oily rag preparatory to greeting him. With a warning slide of his eyes towards the other mechanic, Calmet said loudly:

"I need to have my car painted."

Lazar took his cue quickly:

"But it looks like a brand new car."

"Ah, you know how it is. I got it and my wife doesn't like the colour."

Lazar turned away and led the way to his office:

"Come. I will show you some colour charts."

As they walked into the office, Fortuit, who remained sitting in the car, did not take his eyes off the other mechanic, who got quietly on with his work. He had glanced only casually at Calmet as he talked to Lazar.

As soon as the door to Lazar's office was closed, Calmet dropped his casual tone and his face resumed its normal grim expression:

"Lazar, we're planning to bring in a large shipment of morphine on the night of the eighteenth. Delivery will be made to you between three and four on the following morning."

Lazar's whole thin body shook like a single bowstring as he nodded:

"How much?"

"Enough for you to be able to produce about four hundred kilo of heroin."

Lazar whistled his surprise:

"That means extra men and larger pots."

"That's your problem," shrugged Calmet. "Okay. I think that's it. We'd better go back and have a look at the car to make it look good. Who is the new man?"

Lazar shrugged:

"Business is booming. I needed a new mechanic. I asked the local employment office and they sent him along. He's a mechanic alright—a very good one. I don't think I have anything to worry about there."

Calmet snapped:

"Well, that's another problem. You can't take too much care. I hope you are right."

From the tone of his voice, Lazar felt a shiver of fear down his spine. There was no softness in Calmet, he was completely ruthless, a smaller reflection of his master.

The two men went out and had a quick look round the car. Calmet opened the passenger door to get in, turned at the last moment and snapped:

"Can you do it."

Lazar knew precisely to what he referred:

"Well, if you want to spend money, I'm sure we can arrange to do the job."

"Remember, it has to be the eighteenth."

"It'll be ready," said Lazar. "I'll have the colour mixed."

He walked away to go back to his work on the car he had been inspecting when Calmet and Fortuit arrived. Fortuit started the car, backed it out of the yard and up the slope at the side of the garage. Here, a large window was set in the wall of the garage and, as Calmet gave an abrupt hand signal, he stopped the car and the two men glanced back into the workshop and the yard through this window. The fat mechanic had left his task and now waddled to the side wall of the workshop, on which hung a pay phone. As they watched him, he inserted a coin, picked up the receiver and dialed.

The two men in the car exchanged glances. Fortuit asked:

"Shall I deal with him?"

Calmet shook his head, frowning:

"No, not for the moment—but he will have to be watched. His call could be quite innocent. If he is, then this is the wrong moment to clutter things up with an unnecessary killing."

Reluctantly, Fortuit nodded, put the car back into gear and started the turn to regain the road and go back to the villa.

Johnny Deray put his foot on the accelerator as it rounded the corner that led to the gates of the villa, and shot past, as if he was preparing to drive on to the vague direction of the Riviera and Italy. A bend further on, he came to an abrupt halt, aimed the car at the side of the road, drove quietly into the brush and settled down to wait; after turning it so that it faced back to Marseilles.

It was just ten minutes to twelve. He waited under the hot sun, buoyed up by nibbling on sandwiches he had purchased at the hotel, and drinking a thermos of hot coffee. He was always of the opinion, in situations like this, that a hot drink was more cooling in hot weather than a cold one.

As the day wore on, Johnny knew that it was not his day. The only car to appear was that containing Fortuit and Calmet, returning from their appointment in Marseilles. As they halted by the gate, they blew their horn only once. After a few moments, the gatekeeper came forward, gun in hand, recognised them and opened the gates so that Fortuit could drive up to the villa. It gave the watcher one negatively helpful piece of information—that there was no special code for getting the gates open—recognition was always the best security in working a gate guard operation of that sort. It followed the old rule that the best forms of security usually turned out to be the simplest.

By mid afternoon, Johnny was more than ready to doze off. The heat had become almost unbearable and he was beginning to succumb to the effects of it added to his tiredness, the result of his prodigious all-night drive. He allowed himself to nod off and, when he awoke, it was nearly dark. He was confident that there had been no further comings and goings. His years in the Congo had taught him to sleep almost with his eyes open, certainly with an ear still awake for an suspicious sound.

He felt refreshed and walked a little as darkness fell. He was back by the car by the time complete darkness had fallen, and it was at about eleven o'clock when his waiting finally received the ironic reward that was to be his lot that day.

He heard the sound of a high powered sports car, approaching very rapidly. At first he thought it would roar past, from the speed at which it was going, but, at the last moment, there came a squeal of brakes as it turned and stopped only inches from the iron gates.

Johnny moved as close as he dared, thanking God for his caution as some special lights were snapped on, bathing the gate area in bright light. As the guard came forward from the gatehouse, Johnny noticed it was a different man. More negative information—frequent changes of the guard meant that Brizard had a good number of men at his disposal at the villa.

Meanwhile, the night man had come forward to inspect the new arrival. The car was the latest Porsche and Johnny quickly recognised the driver from the photograph he had seen of Lucienne Brizard. He cursed himself for his bad judgment. Obviously she was bored with her life earlier in the day than his past expertise allowed for. A thought crossed his mind that perhaps he was getting old—and out of touch with the younger generation. Still, she did like fast cars, and that made her the sort of girl whom Johnny could understand and manipulate.

The gates opened and, with a squeal of tires, the Porsche shot up the drive into the darkness. As the gates closed and the roar of the car died away, Johnny went back to his own car, started up and roared down the road back to Marseilles, planning on a good night's sleep, if he were to be able to effect an introduction to Lucienne the following day.

To play it safe, he wanted to be on watch at the Villa very early the next morning. He just hoped that the girl would get bored quite early on in the day. As he returned to the quayside pensione he had picked as his headquarters, he was not to know that events in Paris were taking a more sinister turn that was going to make the Contract a great deal more complicated—including risks to himself that had never entered his calculations.

CHAPTER SIX

After days of waiting, Steve Ventura received Rita's call as he arrived at his office on the day that Johnny Deray arrived in Marseilles. She sounded nervous and breathless on the phone:

"Steve?"

He felt buoyed up:

"Honey, when will I see you."

There was a silence on the other end of the line, then Rita said:

"Kevin and I are flying to the States with Frank's body this afternoon. There'll be some things to clear up. I don't know when I'll be back to close up the apartment. If I wrote to you, would you do it for me?"

Anxiously he brushed the question aside:

"Of course, I would, but I'd hope you'd be back. I'll come over."

He put down the phone without giving her a chance to argue the point. As he told Sally that he was going out the phone rang again. She picked up the receiver, listened for a moment, then put her hand on the mouthpiece:

"It's Joe Kovakian. He says it's very urgent. He was trying to reach you yesterday, remember."

Steve sighed and reluctantly took the phone:

"Hello, Joe. What is it?"

"I'm in the Algerian sector, near the old railway bridge. Can you get here?"

"Why?"

"I've got an informer. He only wants to speak to you."

Steve cursed under his breath:

"Can't you handle it?"

"No, he wants to speak to the top man—and he wants a thousand dollars."

Steve glanced at his watch:

"Can you hold him till noon?"

"I'll do my best. I'll be in the pissoir by the bridge."

Steve slammed down the receiver and rushed out, without giving Sally another glance. He was lucky enough to pick up a cab right outside the Embassy and rode straight round to Rita's apartment.

There was another cab outside the block, the doors open, luggage being put in by the driver. Steve paid off his cab and ran to the entrance as Rita and Kevin appeared, carrying their hand luggage, ready for the trip:

"Honey, don't worry about those. I'll put them in the taxi."

She hardly glanced at him and he could feel the gulf he had not been prepared to recognise widening between them:

"Don't bother."

"It's no bother, honey."

She handed the small bags to the driver who put them on the front seat beside his seat. Then she turned to Steve:

"Look, I'm late already. Kevin, hurry up."

As Kevin came out carrying two of his toys, Steve turned to him, determined to find Rita's achilles' heel, but helpless in the face of her determination to ignore his compassion:

"Hiya champ."

He turned back to Rita as Kevin merely gave him a nod and ran past to the taxi:

"Have you any idea when you'll be back—I've got to see you again and soon."

Rita shook her head:

"Listen, Steve, I really don't know. I can't think that far ahead. I have so many things to settle at home, first."

Steve let his obvious anxiety overcome his tact:

"How long will that take?"

Rita turned away to where Kevin was running up and down the pavement in some private game of his own:

"Kevin, for heaven's sake get in the back of the cab this minute. I won't take any more nonsense from you."

"Please, Rita." Steve's voice was almost a whine.

She shrugged:

"Steve, don't push me, please. I'll be back perhaps in two or three months—I just don't know."

Steve nodded. He obviously wasn't going to get a better answer than that:

"Okay, I'll come out to the airport with you."

This time, when Rita turned from Kevin to face him, he could read a sort of fear in her eyes and he realised that things were too far gone—she was a stranger to him now, they would never be lovers again. Frank's death had made for a much worse break than his own walkout and her subsequent marriage to Frank had fifteen years before. Her voice was tremulous:

"Please, Steve, let's say goodbye here."

She turned from him quickly and climbed into the taxi, hugging Kevin to her as she got in. The window was down and Steve leant in. His face mirrored his inner pain:

"Honey, we can't say goodbye like this."

"Steve, please."

Steve nodded, recognising that she was winning the argument of the break. He smiled at Kevin, balled his fist and tapped the boy on the chin:

"Hey, Champ, take good care of your mom."

"Yes, Uncle Steve," said the boy dutifully.

He turned back to Rita:

"Listen, honey, I'll call you in the States on Sunday."

She managed a thin smile:

"I'm sorry, Steve. I'll look forward to it. Goodbye."

He leant further in and kissed her on the cheek, then:

"Do you need any money?"

"No. No really, I'm fine. I don't need anything. Goodbye."

As he reluctantly withdrew his head, she snapped at the driver:

"Allons y s'il vous plait."

Steve watched as the cab drove off, taking many of his personal hopes with it. Damn Brizard, damn Johnny, damn the job, damn his desk, he thought. All he wanted at that moment was Rita and to be happy with her. He realised in the back of his mind that it was his own action, pulling Frank Matthews into the operation, which had brought this turn of events about and this made him feel even worse.

Only when the cab had disappeared round the corner did he turn and look for another cab that would take him on to his appointment with Joe Kovakian. Joe was a good agent, usually came up with good informers, but he wished that the man had been able to handle this one on his own. After Frank Matthews death all the good informers would be lying low for a while, saving their own skins, and Steve thought it unlikely that Joe had come up with anything that was special enough to warrant the expenditure of a thousand dollars.

The taxi dropped him by the old railway bridge that marked the entry to the Parisian slum that was known as the Algerian quarter because of the number of itinerant North African workers who had moved to France in the years since the war forming the backbone of casual labour at the huge factory estates that were located in the area. In the centre of the city it was always difficult to forget that Paris was a great industrial city as well as the beautiful capital of a gracious country.

The pissoir was under the girders of the bridge and Steve walked slowly towards it, glancing round to make sure that he was not being followed or observed by any familiar or too interested faces, Joe was standing just inside the entrance of the old iron contraption —an institution peculiarly French, circular and open to the sky. Steve joined him and Kovakian said:

"Hi, Steve, sorry to drag you out like this, but I've struck pay dirt. This is really big."

Steve glared at him:

"Well, it's a hell of a nice place to meet—it better be important or I'll have your ass."

Kovakian looked at his superior with alarm. Steve was an emotional man, but he had seldom seen him in as bad a temper as this. He said firmly:

"It is good."

They didn't speak for a moment as a workman pushed past into the interior of the pissoir, then:

"Well, what have you got?"

"I hit the jackpot."

"Okay, spit it out."

Kovakian led Steve back out onto the street, saying anxiously:

"This is for real—the job that could really nail Brizard once and for all, buddy."

Steve frowned. As far as he was concerned, Brizard was on the verge of being dealt with anyway. Kovakian paused and pointed towards a pillar that was one of the supports of the old bridge. A man with a Mediterranean cast of countenance was lounging against it, wearing faded jeans and a tattered sweater—a seaman perhaps, his nationality anything from Greek and Turkish to North African—his condition, down and out:

"See that man over there."

"What's he got."

Kovakian spoke slowly, savouring his triumph, sure that Steve would react with pleasure at last:

"Only a tip off on the biggest drug smuggling operation into Marseilles for the last couple of decades—and a date when the stuff is coming in—and a connection with Jacques Brizard. Listen, I'll go over and have a word, then you stroll over."

Steve nodded his acquiescence in this strategy and waited while Kovakian strolled slowly over to the informer, who braced up and paid attention as he saw the American coming. Kovakian spoke to the man for a few minutes, then turned round and pointed to Steve. As he did so, he was saying to the informer:

"That man over there by the pissoir. He's the man you have to tell—he's the man with the money."

Steve took the pointing finger as a signal and began to stroll across to the man. He arrived and joined them apparently casually, as far as it would concern any of the people passing by:

"Hi."

"This is Monsieur Minieri," said Kovakian.

The man, who on closer inspection must have been Algerian, said truculently:

"Where's my money?"

This was not a promising beginning and Steve glanced sharply at Kovakian and said:

"He did suggest the deal would be for a thousand dollars."

"Well, let's hear what you've got."

"No money. No information."

Steve sighed and produced his wallet. He took ten one hundred dollar bills from it and held them loosely in his hand so that the man could see it—in fact he kept his eyes fixed on it. Then he turned to Kovakian again:

"Let's get on with this."

Kovakian snapped at the man:

"A shipment leaves Turkey tonight."

"Where for," snapped Kovakian.

"I don't know."

"You knew last night."

The man hesitated for a moment, his eyes flickering from the faces of the two Americans, down to the money and back again. At last, he licked his lips nervously and said:

"Marseilles."

"And when's it due," snapped Kovakian.

Again the Algerian was reluctant:

"On the eighteenth."

"How much?"

"Four hundred kilos."

Steve felt interest for the first time. Until that moment he had thought it was a complete waste of time. Places and dates, but no names. It could be someone who had once been on the edge of the operation and had discovered a way to get some money out of the generous and stupid Americans. But the amount quoted—if it could be believed—was huge, whatever it was:

"Four hundred kilos of what?"

"Morphine base."

Kovakian and Steve glanced at one another, Kovakian waiting for a sign of approval, Steve giving it with his eyes, but in the same time transmitting his surprise and disbelief at the enormous size of the shipment. Kovakian took up the questioning again:

"Who's the buyer?"

The Algerian shrugged:

"I don't know."

Kovakian, who had been showing increasing signs of impatience at the man's reluctance to tell Steve what he had so eagerly talked about the night before, leaned forward and grabbed the man, jerking him up, so that his feet were off the ground in a second. A sudden flash of fear showed in his eyes:

"You knew Goddam well who it was last night."

Steve took his cue and acted like the nice guy on the interrogation team. He tapped Joe on the shoulder:

"No, Joe. No muscle talk. Monsieur Minieri is only any good to us if he wants to tell us what he knows, not if you want to force something out of him. He'd give us any name you wanted to get himself off the hook like that."

Kovakian relaxed and let go of the man, who stepped back until he had the pillar at his back and watched the two men warily. Steve said politely:

"I'm sorry about that, my colleague is a little impulsive. Now, tell me, who's the buyer?"

The man took a deep breath and licked his lips—in fear rather than greed this time. It was as if he knew that the information could sign his own death warrant. At last:

"Brizard."

"Jacques Brizard?"

"Yes, Monsieur, Jacques Brizard."

In the tenement above the concourse that ran under the old railway bridge, the man on the top floor balcony lowered his high-powered binoculars and laughed softly. Lip reading was a special skill he had mastered and Brizard and Calmet paid him well for the skill. He picked up the phone that was by his elbow and went through the frustrating business of calling Marseilles. When the receiver was finally picked up, it was Calmet who answered, at Brizard's villa. He just said:

"Minieri has talked."

"Good," said Calmet. "Keep him under observation. Tell him that he has to be back in Marseilles by train the day after tomorrow."

The man replaced the receiver and picked up his binoculars again to catch the end of the three man conversation far below him. In Marseilles, he knew that Calmet would be reporting to Brizard and the machine to protect the crime boss would swing quickly into action. He had primed the machine but could now sit back and wait for the results without being in any way involved.

Ventura was still asking his questions, but the source was drying up now, genuinely running out of information:

"Marseilles is a big city. Have you any idea where the drop will be on the eighteenth?"

The man shrugged:

"I don't know."

"You don't know," echoed Steve, shrugging in his turn. He believed the man and handed over the thousand dollars which was snatched from his hand and disappeared into his jeans pocket in one swift movement. Steve said:

"Listen, if you find out where the drop will be, there's another thousand in it for you."

The man nodded, then darted past the two Americans and disappeared across the road between two tenement buildings. Steve turned, amused by the man's sudden caution and shrugged at Kovakian:

"Well, do you think we'll see him again. He didn't seem too sure of himself on the details."

Kovakian bridled:

"You'd certainly see me for another thousand dollars."

Steve shook his head:

"I don't think so. Brizard's too clever to let too much of the information out to many people, but it's good information nonetheless."

"You bet," said Kovakian enthusiastically. "You've got the place and you've got the date—you've got the buyer—all you have to do now is pick him up. The job's practically been done for you."

Steve laughed bitterly from the previous experience of Brizard's slippery luck:

"Yeah, all I have to do is pick him up."

They walked in silence for a while, as the implications of the information sunk in on Steve. If the information was anything like correct it was, though he would never admit it to Kovakian, the strongest information he had ever had on Jacques Brizard; the closest he had ever come to being able to nail him—and he was not over-optimistic, this was one on which he really could nail the gang boss. It was only then that he remembered Johnny Deray and his fifty thousand dollar job and he cursed inwardly—far better to put Brizard in jail for the rest of his life, rather than kill him. The latter might bring things to a halt for the moment but, sooner or later, someone like Calmet would pick up the pieces of the operation and have the intelligence and discipline to make it work again—but if Brizard was in jail, then they would be able to pick up the whole network—in the countries of the growing and export as well as in the refineries of Marseilles and the surrounding area before they went off to the retail pushers round the world.

Steve was just coming to the conclusion that he must find a way to stop Johnny, at least until after the eighteenth and their chance to nail Brizard, when Kovakian pulled a handful of change from his pocket, looked at it, then stopped. Steve stopped too and looked at him, his eyebrows raised interrogatively:

"Well?"

"There's enough change here to buy us both a drink."

Steve shrugged dismissively:

"Where the hell would you and I go where it would be safe to be seen with each other?"

Despite the offensiveness of the remark, Kovakian could see the sense in this and nodded:

"I'll call you, then."

Steve nodded:

"Thanks, Joe."

They split up and went their separate ways. Steve walked in to the first cafe he found and went to the pay phone on the wall. He rang the Sureté and asked for Inspector Briac, cursing and slamming down the receiver when he was told that Briac was not in for the moment.

He was suddenly worried, having convinced himself that Johnny would have to be stopped. He rang Sally and said that if anyone called he would be at his apartment. He got a cab straight back and ran into the apartment as he heard the phone ring. It was Briac:

"I had a message, Mr. Ventura. You want to speak to me."

"Yes. Urgent. Notre Dame Bridge. Thirty minutes." He slammed down the receiver before the policeman had time to reply.

Steve went straight to the bridge and waited impatiently for the policeman to arrive. His fears made his mind as overcast as the leaden sky above. Briac arrived dead on time, the smile on his face as usual as Steve glowered at him. He said:

"Well, what was so urgent?"

"Hi, did you hear anything about Deray?"

"Deray?"

Steve glowered:

"Don't come the innocent with me."

Briac shrugged:

"Alright, but be careful. Officially, I can know nothing about our little scheme."

Steve nodded:

"Sorry. But that's what I called you about. I'm cancelling the contract, can you recall Deray?"

Briac expressed surprise by the expression on his face, but his voice was steady, not anxiously inquisitive:

"I see. May I ask why?"

Steve shrugged:

"Let's just say I've changed my mind. I'll get Jacques Brizard some other way."

"How?"

"That's a good question. Anyway, that's beside the point at the moment. I want you to call Marseilles and have Deray picked up and taken out of circulation until we can cancel."

"On what charge?"

Steve shrugged:

"I don't care, robbery, murder. Just find some way to stop him."

Briac sighed:

"That's not easy."

"What do you mean?"

"Well, to start with, as a policeman I cannot give false information to my colleagues."

Steve slapped his hands together:

"But you can recommend a professional assassin for a job? Don't argue—make the call and stop Deray."

Briac could see that the other man was deadly serious and it would be unwise for him to argue further. As he watched Steve, the latter turned and walked away. Briac himself turned and walked away, his mind working fast. He had reasons of his own for wondering why Johnny Deray's services were no longer required, for Steve's priming of the killer would have solved some of Inspector Briac's crime problems as well.

As for Steve, he prayed that Johnny could be stopped. If necessary he was sure that the other man would take up the challenge again later. Still no harm would have been done yet. Johnny wouldn't even have reached Marseilles, never mind have got some sort of line to Brizard. No, on the whole, he was relieved in his conscience and excited by the new prospect of nailing Brizard once and for all. He could not know how muddied the waters of the Brizard affair were about to become.

CHAPTER SEVEN

Unaware of the storm that was breaking around his plans, Johnny Deray was at his post up the road from the entrance to the Brizard villa shortly after nine o'clock the following morning. He had chosen a driving outfit that looked conspicuously expensive without in any way being flashy and obvious. A girl as rich as Lucienne would always notice things like that. He also wore casual leather driving gloves, another sign of the true sports car enthusiast.

He was relieved that he did not have long to wait. The day before had been an uncomfortable waste of time and something told him that he had to get into the Brizard household quickly—that this was not an assassination job that could be carefully planned for over months of detail. Jacques Brizard was a walking security layout and the only way through his defences was the frontal assault.

The gates of the villa opened and the little Porsche slid out onto the road and turned towards Marseilles, travelling slowly. Johnny ran back to his car, got in, started off and roared after her. It took a few minutes to catch up with her and, as he roared round a bend in the road, he was relieved to see that she was alone and he could put his plan into effect.

Lucienne Brizard adjusted her rear view mirror and

almost automatically accelerated as she saw the sleek brown Alfa roaring up behind her. It was a lovely machine, more than the equal of hers, but her blood pumped with excitement as she thought, given a race, she could show the driver a trick or two, especially as she knew the road so well.

As the Alfa pulled out to pass her, the driver blowing his horn, she realised that she was going to get the chance to show her paces. She shifted suddenly into a lower gear and pressed the accelerator down onto the floor. She saw the driver of the other car smile as she sped ahead.

As for Johnny he was relieved that his instincts had proved correct. If his driving technique was good as he thought it, then he would have her eating out of his hand in no time. He too changed down and put heavy pressure on the accelerator. The Alfa roared past the girl's Porsche, then he changed up, slowing down so that she was forced to brake. Lucienne had been expecting this trick and her reflexes worked as well as the engine of her car. She pulled out and passed the Alfa almost before Johnny realised it. As she went past, she slowed slightly to inspect her rival and was pleased with what she saw. A man who was young, but not too young, with good strong features, clear eyes and a shock of blond hair. If they both survived the sport, Lucienne felt she could be very interested in this man. Her car took her ahead and she adjusted her mind back on to the road.

Deray had brought the Alfa up again and as the two cars screamed round the next bend, almost neck and neck, they saw a saloon car in front of them, travelling slowly in the same direction and too slow to get out of the way. Johnny made an instant decision to leave the road to Lucienne and abruptly went on to the sand embankment as she shot past on the clear road. When the car was passed, Lucienne was ahead by about a car's length. She smiled as she checked her rear view mirror. She had beaten him with this trick, but his handling of his car had been good enough to earn more respect from her during the rest of the contest.

This was on them almost at once. The road took a right hand bend, with a wide flat sandy outcrop on the right. As Lucienne went round it, Johnny switched to a low gear and charged across the sand, coming back onto the road with a superbly controlled skid just ahead of her, causing her to change up and slow her car, thus losing any advantage the road gave her. Johnny could have surged ahead at that point, but a race was not his game, so he slowed up in his turn, so that Lucienne, taken by surprise by his tactics—not realising that he was playing to win something other than a car race—surged past. As she went by she gave him a smile and a wave which he was only too pleased to return.

From his previous journeys, Johnny knew that they would soon be reaching the long, wide straight that led to the outskirts of Marseilles and the marina and yacht club. He had to pull something out of the bag before then, so he now concentrated on a speed pass. This took him two bends and a confrontation with a juggernaut lorry which almost gave him other things to worry about besides his driving, before he came alongside again, signalled the nearness of the accident to her by fanning himself with one hand, then pressed ahead.

The two cars came round the bend and on to the long straight, with its high, flat, sand embankments. Johnny slammed on his brakes and Lucienne shot round him. The abruptness of the manoeuvre she had to perform caused her car to spin right round under the nose of his and go off the road, sending up a spume of sand as she righted it, her face now set and angry. Johnny had the inspiration to follow suit, moving round her again and accelerating as he spun the wheel so that the car performed a parabola in front of the Porsche, throwing up another arc of sand. Soon both cars were spinning down the verge performing movements that were almost ballectic in their precision as they flung sand up from under their tires at one another.

Soon they would be at the end of the stretch. Lucienne was going to the yacht club, so, with a final wide parabola, she straightened up back onto the road, turned the corner at top speed, zoomed down the empty street and pulled up abruptly at the yacht club kerb. Following her, Johnny was caught unawares and zoomed past. Ahead he had some two hundred yards of road and the whole width of the Mediterranean. He did the only thing he could under these conditions—slammed on the brakes and, at the same moment, spun the wheel. The Alfa, responding superbly to the signal, went sideways across the road and came to a perfect slalom halt. Johnny switched off the engine. Lucienne had climbed out of the Porsche and was staring in alarm at the direction he had taken. He jumped from the car and gave her a low bow. Her response was to hold up her hands in an imitation of applause, then she beckoned him back. He got back into the car, turned and drove to park it next to hers. When he got out, she was at his side:

"Bonjour, Monsieur."

Johnny gave her a mock bow:

"Bonjour Madamoiselle."

Lucienne glanced round and laughed:

"As there seems to be no one around to introduce us, I suggest we remedy the situation for ourselves. My name is Lucienne Brizard."

Johnny took her hand:

"Johnny Davos."

"That was a lovely piece of driving, Mr. Davos."

"I must return the compliment."

The two cars received minute inspection and comparison from the alternative drivers, then Lucienne asked:

"Look, are you doing anything for lunch?"

Johnny grinned:

"I wasn't, but I think it might be booked now." He accompanied the hint with a charming wink and Lucienne laughed:

"Mr. Davos, I must assume you are not a member of the yacht club or I would have seen you here before. Come inside. I think we could both do with a drink—and I don't think you'll be disappointed with the food."

As they ate their meal inside the huge comfortable restaurant with its glass-walled view out to sea, Johnny probed quietly, trying to find out Lucienne's tastes and weaknesses. When he had discovered them, he felt that she was not the sort of girl he would have chosen for himself, but she was beautiful enough for him to look forward to the liaison he was going to bring about with her.

Lucienne Brizard was a girl who suffered from a disease that was common to many of the very rich—she was used to having her own way—and would only respond to a man if he made it seem as if it was her idea. Anything that did not interest her from the first moment would be dismissed at once as not worth a second glance. Well, if that was the way she operated, then Johnny was going to lie back and enjoy it.

He remained cool and detached and, whenever possible during the meal, he turned the conversation back to talk about sports cars—nothing heavy, but polite, as if he assumed that was her chief interest. As they lingered over coffee he used an old joke that never failed on girls who liked cars:

"This friend of mine. He has a 56 Mercedes 300 SL—you remember the gullwing."

She frowned:

"The gullwing?"

"You must know the one—you climb into it with the door on the top."

"Oh yes," laughed Lucienne. "It was a beautiful car to handle, I tried one. But it is so hot in the summer."

Johnny nodded:

"No ventilation. So he spent a fortune putting in an efficient air-conditioning unit, but there was only one problem."

"Which was?"

"Once he got the unit in, he couldn't get in the car himself."

As Lucienne laughed, throwing her head back and revealing a flawless white neck, the waiter came over with a plate on which was folded the bill. Johnny leant over to take the bill, but Lucienne got her hand to it first:

"Cash is not allowed—it's the rule here. All accounts must be signed. As you are not a member—yet—you cannot sign the bill."

Johnny acknowledged her logic with an inclination of his head, which also hid the involuntary smirk of triumph at hearing the word 'yet'—she had taken the bait alright. Now it was just a question of playing along, knowing when to say yes and when to dig his heels in and say no without precipitating a crisis of rejection. It was a thin line with girls like Lucienne. He laughed:

"What time's dinner, then, if I don't have to pay."

"Come early for cocktails."

He pretended that he did not quite understand:

"I was joking."

"I wasn't."

"Well, then," Johnny rose. "I'll see you here at dinner."

Lucienne laughed:

"Oh, no, not here. I meant at my father's villa. He would be delighted to meet you."

"Your father's villa?"

"Yes. It's on the coast road, the big gates just before you caught up with me. It's the only house out that way—my father is fond of his privacy. Shall we say seven o'clock for cocktails. Dinner is habitually at eight. We have a very fine chef and my father doesn't like to keep him waiting."

Johnny smiled:

"Then he must be good. Chefs with an urge for punctuality are very rare these days. I will remember to be on time."

They walked out of the club, back to their cars. Johnny was about to climb into the Alfa, when he turned:

"By the way, how do I dress?"

Lucienne laughed:

"Anything you're comfortable in."

He smiled:

"Really? I think I've got the very thing—but I won't wear that as I would hate to offend the chef."

He climbed into the car, slammed the door, waved as he started the car and then zoomed away.

He drove round the corner, then disappeared into the maze of side streets as soon as he was out of sight. His hotel was only two streets away from the yacht club and it wouldn't do for Lucienne to go past and see the Alfa parked outside such a place. He left it in one of the side streets and made his way cautiously back to the hotel and his room.

He rested for the afternoon and then showered and dressed. He picked Chelsea boots for the evening's entertainment, a good, dark cut suit—with a jacket that he had had specially made so that it would not show an extra bulge. Into the left boot he slipped a small hand gun and he wore his armpit holster with another useful weapon in it. It wouldn't do to be caught unawares—it would give him a chance if his cover was blown by Jacques Brizard's first enquiries. Not that he intended to finish the Brizard job so quickly, he was too much of an artist for that. It would have to be done in such a way that not even 'Johnny Davos' could have done it. But you never knew when you were going to run into someone you knew, someone who had met you before. There was no one in the file who fitted the bill, but you never knew.

He drove in a leisurely fashion out to the villa, arriving at the gatehouse just before seven. Though he was aware of the routine, he had to act as if he wasn't, so he went right up to the gates, hooted with quick impatience, then got out of the car as if he was going to open them himself. He feigned surprise when the gateman, his rifle under his arm, appeared:

"Yes, Sir?" At least the man was polite. That didn't often go with security guards. Jacques Brizard obviously trained his men well.

"My name is Davos. Miss Lucienne Brizard is expecting me."

"One moment, please, Sir."

The man walked back to the gatehouse and picked up an internal phone. He talked for a moment, replaced the receiver and lumbered back to press the button that opened the gates. Johnny jumped back into the car and drove through with a polite nod.

When he arrived a few minutes later outside the

huge front entrance to the villa, Lucienne was waiting for him on the steps to take him inside:

"Hello."

She was dressed in a long evening gown, which covered her legs to the ground and compensated by leaving her perfect shoulders bare and showing a generous glimpse of a well-rounded bosom. He paused on the steps to drink her in and said, in an admiring voice:

"Well, Hi."

"Come in." She turned and he followed her into the villa. Inside, she led him down the corridor to the dining room. As he glanced round he saw the discreetly arranged television cameras. Mr. Brizard was indeed well-protected. Lucienne said:

"Was the villa as easy to find as I said it would be?"

Johnny laughed:

"Well, the grounds were easy, it was the house that I found hard to locate once I was inside."

Lucienne laughed:

"My father's very anxious to meet you."

She led him through the dining room, with its quota of cameras in the corners of the room and out onto the terrace.

He recognised Jacques Brizard at once, tall, distinguished, a man in well-kept middle-age. Next to him was a chic woman who obviously didn't have a brain in her head—that must be the mistress. There was another couple, obviously guests and Johnny was quick to note an obvious gunman standing by the portable bar.

As Lucienne and Johnny moved forward, Jacques Brizard excused himself from the others and came over, his arm outstretched. The two men shook hands and Brizard said:

"Welcome to my house. You must be Mr. Davos."

"How do you do, Sir."

He turned to the other couple:

"Count, Countess, May I present Mr. John Davos. The Count and Countess Dorville."

They three of them exchanged bows, then the other woman came forward. Johnny had seen the look on many a face. That could mean trouble. The woman was eating him up with her eyes, and casting envious glances at Lucienne. To encounter feminine jealousy in a set-up like this might upset the whole apple cart. Johnny made a mental note to move the affair forward faster than he had originally anticipated. It might have the effect of putting this other woman off, if it became obvious very quickly that he was wrapped up in Lucienne, that might do the trick.

Brizard became aware of his mistress's stare:

"Oh, I'm sorry, my dear. Madame Apcar, Mr. Davos." He turned to Lucienne: "My darling, I am sure your friend could do with a drink after his drive from Marseilles."

"Straight scotch would do nicely, thanks."

Lucienne went over to the bar as Brizard asked:

"Are you visiting Marseilles for business or pleasure, Mr. Davos?"

"Well, both really."

"I hope that you will be rewarded with a profitable trip on both levels."

Johnny fought hard to keep his face straight, the irony out of his voice. Life paid dividends with little jokes like this:

"Thank you, Mr. Brizard. I'm sure that it will be."

As he spoke, he moved round Brizard so that he was now close to the bar as Lucienne turned with his drink. He took it:

"Thank you."

In more senses of the word than one. As she moved

aside, he saw that there was a gun stashed under the bar—just where Wilson would be able to get at it in a hurry if there was any trouble.

Dinner was a huge success, both for Johnny and the effect he was having on the others. It was near the end of the meal before the reason for the other guests became apparent. It seemed that Jacques Brizard's public face that year was set against pollution of the environment—in particular the pollution of the Mediteranean. To this end he was holding a huge ball at the largest hotel in Marseilles on the eighteenth of the month—and it was important that the Count and Countess Dorville attend—to set the social seal on the occasion.

At the end of the meal, Brizard started sounding off on the subject of pollution—and the crime committed by human beings in their roles as tamers of the environment:

"Man is in a terrible way," he pontificated. "A terrible way. Not content with polluting our own habitat, we are now attempting to contaminate outer space. It's true the earth, the sea, the very air we breathe is no longer good. Soon there will be nothing left for our children to enjoy. We are killing tomorrow."

Johnny thought this was quite a good slogan, especially from France's number one killer, who ordered the death of little innocent people all over the world, every day. The Countess was much moved by her host's homily:

"My goodness, Jacques, what a terrible picture you paint."

Brizard nodded, sadly:

"These are terrible times we live in. It is not only the deterioration of the environment but the deterioration of the quality of our very lives that is at stake." He paused and glanced towards Lucienne, as if seeking her encouragement that he was taking the right line, before continuing:

"That is why I am calling this year's charity ball, Survival 74."

The Countess clapped her hands together, overcome by his eloquence and seemingly excited by the prospect as if the fighting against pollution was a physical war:

"Bravo, Mr. Brizard, Jacques. You will certainly have whole-hearted support from myself and my husband—and a suitable donation."

"Yes, dear," muttered the Count, who didn't look as entirely happy as his wife.

The Countess now had the floor and she decided to draw out Johnny who had so far been blessed by not being included into the conversation:

"Are you interested in survival, Mr. Davos."

Johnny smiled, both for the assembled company and for his own inner amusement:

"I never think of anything else, Countess."

"But which part of the environmental problem concerns you the most?"

Johnny's answer came quickly:

"Over-population."

Before the Countess could ask Johnny to expand on his answer, Brizard, who sensed the conversation was going into dangerous channels from the point of view of his donations, leant forward:

"A very interesting angle, Mr. Davos. Did you know that at the time of Jesus Christ there were about a hundred million people in the world. In the seventeenth century there were five hundred million people and in a few years there will be as many as—."

The Countess cut across his statistics:

"All those ghastly people—how horrible."

Madame Apcar dropped in her two cents worth to Johnny's amusement, though the others took her at the face value of her remark:

"People will always make love. What is the solution?"

"Not birth control or abortion, I trust," said the Countess.

Lucienne, irritated with the way in which her father had cut across Johnny, and considering that he was doing fine and not upsetting the charity ball applecart, turned to him:

"Is that what you had in mind?"

Johnny waited until he considered that he had everyone's attention, then:

"Oh no, nothing like that."

He paused and it was Lucienne who supplied the cue:

"Then what?"

"I think that some people should be killed."

The effect was not quite universally what he had been aiming at. While the Count, Countess and Madame Apcar looked shocked, Jacques Brizard's face showed no reaction and Lucienne threw back her head and laughed:

"Yes, but which ones."

"The bad ones."

The Countess, frowning, leant forward:

"But who would be the judge of which people were good and which were bad, Mr. Davos."

"Why me, of course."

Brizard beamed down the table at him:

"Otherwise they might choose you."

The tension that Johnny's suggestion had slowly built up round the table as to whether his suggestion was serious or frivolous, was pricked immediately and Johnny happily joined in with the general laughter.

Lucienne leant over and smiled, she was happy that she had thought to invite him to dinner, he was doing very well. She knew all the signs; it was not often that her father warmed to one of her friends—but then it was not often that she brought home a man as worldly and assured as Johnny.

Shortly after this exchange, Brizard rose as a signal that the dinner party was at an end. The Count and Countess accepted an invitation to go to his library to look at his collection of coins, but Lucienne pulled Johnny back from the group as they went along the corridor:

"I've something better for us to do."

Johnny raised one eyebrow questioningly:

"I don't think your father would like that. Anyway, I'd like to see the coins. I'm very interested in money."

"It's not what you think," smiled Lucienne. "That's for later. Come on."

She took his hand and led him back towards the dining room. Just before the dining room door there was a flight of steps that led downwards—on the way in, Johnny had assumed that this was the way to the kitchen—and Lucienne hustled him down them. At the bottom she said:

"This is what Daddy calls my games room. He thinks it keeps me at home more often."

Johnny looked round and whistled. He was in a huge room, probably under a good two-thirds of the villa, equipped with table tennis, card tables, a static bicycle and all the paraphernalia of the normal gym—but, in addition to that, there was a complete bowling alley with four lanes at one end of the room. Lucienne watched his face, then laughed:

"I'm glad we've got something to impress you."

Johnny said:

"How's your bowling?"

She walked forward eagerly:

"Best of five?"

"Okay."

They walked over to the dispenser and Lucienne turned the knob that switched on the machinery that put the alley into normal working order. Johnny flipped a coin and Lucienne called. It was heads and she bowled first. He noticed with some alarm that only one pin was left standing. She obviously got a lot of practice in spite of her sneer about 'the Games Room'.

He picked up his bowl and was moving forward as the pins were mechanically replaced when Lucienne said:

"Hey, aren't you going to take your jacket off."

With the gun under his armpit, there was only one way Johnny could play it. He paused, looking as if his concentration on the game had been unforgiveably interrupted, and said:

"No."

There was no answer to an answer as blunt as that, but Lucienne protested weakly:

"Oh, come on. You can't be that good."

Johnny grinned:

"Now that is not the same subject. Anyway, that's for me to know and you to find out."

He turned and bowled—and was relieved that he too only left one pin standing at the end of the alley—mind you, he knew this was more by luck than judgement.

After five bowls they were still even and Johnny could not deny that he was impressed. Lucienne wanted to go on and, after an initial show of reluctance, accompanied by glances at his watch, Johnny allowed himself to be apparently persuaded. In fact, at that moment, wild horses would not have driven him away. Inside, in spite of the act he was putting on in his efforts to snare the girl, he felt angry; felt that she had presented him with a real challenge. He had a rising feeling that his masculinity was being questioned and he had to win.

Four more bowls each and honours were still even. As Lucienne was about to take her fifth bowl, Johnny said:

"After this one, I really have to go. Look at the time."

It did the trick. Lucienne obviously had other plans for him later and her irritation that these might not work put her slightly out of her stride as she threw her ball down. Three pins were missed in the slaughter. It was just the edge he needed and he took his bowl with a cool, controlled hand, knocking down all the pins. Lucienne's face was a study as he turned, smiling, to her. She didn't much like being beaten by anybody—particularly a man. Still, now was the moment to flatter her—as an expert congratulating a good amateur:

"You're really very good at the game, Lucienne. You have just the right spinning throw."

"So are you," she breathed.

He shrugged:

"It's nothing really. You should see me tap dance."

She walked over to him and put her arms round his neck, pressing herself up against him, letting the length of her body press through her thin dress to entice and trap him. He kissed her on the forehead, took her arms and firmly pushed her away. She coloured angrily, particularly as he still maintained his attractive smile:

"What's the matter?"

Johnny pointed to the television camera that was strategically planted in a corner of the ceiling as it had been in all the other rooms he had entered:

"I never make love on TV. It's always been a rule with me and I don't intend to change it now."

Lucienne took his hand:

"I'm sorry. Let's go into the garden."

He smiled back at her encouragingly and asked:

"What are they all for anyway?"

"We have to have them all over the house," sighed Lucienne. "They're for insurance. You get used to them after a while."

Johnny laughed:

"It's when you get used to them that you have to watch out. Remember what happens to politicians who install automatic tape recorders. Still, you can't be too careful, can you sunshine?" This last sally was directed at a piece of grotesque sculpture that stood in the corridor at the head of the steps to the games room—a piece which Johnny recognised and knew was worth at least a million francs.

They walked through the dining room and out onto the deserted terrace. From there they stepped down onto the lawn. In the night light of a dim moon, Johnny could see the silver edge of the sea at the end of the lawn. They walked down the lawn, Lucienne leading him away to the left, until they were in a small summer house in the darkness. If there was a television camera suitably installed, Johnny could not see it in the dark.

Lucienne turned and pressed herself close to him. The feel and perfume of her were very tempting, but tonight was the night for rejection. If he made things too easy for her, then she would not be really interested in him, and a continuing relationship was important. He was in no way afraid of the quality of performance he would give—he was yet to find a dissatisfied customer—but things that came too easily to someone like Lucienne were likely to be put aside.

He kissed her hard on the mouth and their tongues fought a brief encounter as she tried to press herself through his suit. She stepped back suddenly in the darkness:

"Ouch—what's that in your side."

She had obviously pressed herself rather hard against the gun and Johnny laughed in the dark:

"Sorry, I'm carrying some special metal plates in my pocket. There wasn't time to get rid of them before I came out."

He expected more questions and had no answer for them. He was relieved when she giggled and said that she'd be a little more careful this time. Once more they embraced and Johnny knew that, at that moment, he could have done anything he wanted with her, but even so, he pushed her away:

"Now, I really must be going."

Lucienne was obviously hurt:

"What's wrong this time?"

"Just the time—and the place. Some other time, I'll show you how to deal with the cameras—unless you can come back to my hotel."

"No," she said quickly. "I can't do that—not to-night."

They walked back across the lawn in silence and into the house. Brizard was sitting in his study, the door open and they went in so that Johnny could thank him for dinner and say goodnight. If Johnny had drawn his gun at that moment, Brizard would have been a dead man, and there was a good chance for him to get away—to the seawards side if not via the main gate and the fences. But this was not the way Johnny worked—that would be hit or miss, not a good professional job. Anyway, his pride would be hurt if, after his careful manipulation, he didn't enjoy himself with Lucienne.

Brizard rose and shook his hand with every indication of welcoming warmth:

"It has been nice to meet you, Mr. Davos. I hope that you will come here again during your visit."

"It would be my pleasure, Mr. Brizard."

He turned and Lucienne accompanied him to the front door. He noticed out of the corner of his eye that the red light was glowing on top of the camera that covered the front door, which meant that Brizard was watching—and probably listening—to them.

Lucienne kissed him with promising affection:

"Have lunch with me tomorrow at the club."

Johnny thought for a moment, as if he was running a series of appointments through his mind, then:

"Fine, but this time I pay." And this time, he thought, I find a cleverer way of keeping a gun on me.

She kissed him again:

"I'll see you at one."

He walked down the steps, got in his car and, as he drove off, he flashed his lights and waved at her as she stood at the top of the steps. As he went down the drive to the main gate, he felt satisfied. It had been a very promising evening. Now, barring accidents, the way ahead was clear for him. It was just a question of cementing the relationship and setting up Brizard from there. He speculated that Brizard was more possessive about his daughter than any other of his possessions—that should provide good leverage when the time came.

In the house, Brizard waited at the study door for his daughter:

"Lucienne, would you like a night cap before bed."

"No thanks, Father."

"The dinner, did you think it went well—will the charity ball be a success."

She laughed:

"Oh, Father, you were perfect. You have a silver tongue. You don't need my opinion, you could talk blood out of a stone."

"So could your new friend." He kissed her gently on the forehead, then went back into the study.

Sitting at his desk, he waited a moment, then switched the TV on to the upstairs corridor. Lucienne was just going into her room. He snapped off the picture and sound, then picked up one of his phones—a private line with a blank face. It had been an expensive installation but it provided him with a private open line to Calmet's apartment in Marseilles—in one of the buildings that his own construction company had built.

Calmet, ever-faithful and ever-waiting, picked up the receiver at his end almost at once:

"Yes, Mr. Brizard?"

"I want you to check on somebody. John Davos. Six foot, blond, blue eyes. Drives a new Alfa Romeo. Brown. About thirty-five but looks younger. I want to know everything about him—especially if he sails close to the wind, as I suspect."

"Do we try the special contact?"

Brizard hesitated for a moment:

"Only if we have to. Try the usual channels for the first enquiries and let me know as soon as you've dug anything up."

"Yes, Sir. There is another matter."

"What?"

"The new mechanic—Fournier is his name—at Lazar's garage. We think he's a police informer."

"Deal with it—permanently." Brizard slammed down the phone and went to bed a contented man. Calmet had never let him down.

CHAPTER EIGHT

In Marseilles, the main vegetable market of the old town is located in the Place de Lenche. From shortly after dawn it is a place full of bustle and activity where, amid all the crowds that are moving around trading in wholesale and stall vegetables, men can meet without exciting any particular attention. It is an area through which traffic cannot pass, except on one road along the edge of the market, a narrow road squeezed between the open area and a row of old houses of the picturesque type that place Marseilles as an extension of the south of France. Most of the rest of the city looks like a huge commercial and industrial centre of the type that can be found all over Europe regardless of location.

It was just after seven o'clock on the morning after Johnny Deray had made his first foray into the security-sealed household of his target, Jacques Brizard, that a fat man with a moustache lumbered into the market and went to sit on a bench next to the railing that separated the market place from the road. He was waiting for the meeting that he had called and arranged the night before. The man was Fournier, the new mechanic at the garage of Lazar, the chief refining chemist of Brizard's drug operation—his contact was going to be a policeman and he felt nervous and excited with the information he had to impart. The crowd was not as big as he would have liked but after nervously glancing round two or three times he was pretty sure that he was not being observed.

He spotted Inspector Farjas of the Marseilles police as soon as the man came into the market from an alley on the far side of the open area. He did not make directly for his informer, but stopped at one of the fruit and vegetable stalls, looked through the wares that were on view and, at last, ordered half a kilo of ripe tomatoes.

These were weighed and bagged for him and, as Fournier watched and waited with rising impatience, the Inspector paid and waited for his change. Only then did he stroll slowly over to where Fournier was seated. He sat a little way down the bench, put the bag between the two men, opened it, took out a tomato and began to suck the juice from it. At the same time, Fournier saw him drop some folded bills into the top of the bag, between the tomatoes.

For the first time he looked up at the nervous informer, but he did not speak. At last Fournier nervously licked his lips to answer the unasked question about the information he had:

"A large shipment is scheduled to arrive in Marseilles from Turkey on the eighteenth."

"Where?"

Fournier shrugged:

"That I don't know."

Inspector Farjas nodded. The information on the date was valuable enough and he knew that any informer in Marseilles who reported on Jacques Brizard's operation was taking his life in his hands. He was lucky to get anything at all.

"Are you sure it's the eighteenth."

"Yes, Calmet told Lazar."

"So the chemist's involved." That was something. That meant that one of a dozen houses could eventually receive the raw drug for refining. There was a chance that if the department moved quickly enough —and if the leaks could be kept plugged before the operation—the drugs could be taken out of circulation. Even if their owner went scot-free he would be out of pocket.

"I have nothing more," said Fournier.

The Inspector nodded:

"Thank you."

He got up and walked briskly away, back through the crowd and down the alley up which he had come, to where a police driver was waiting to take him back to the station.

Fournier sat alone on the bench for a while. He took no notice of the car that came slowly down the road behind him. It stopped almost directly behind the bench and the back window on his side was wound down. Henri, one of Brizard's men, was driving and Kurt was seated at the back window. He called out:

"Fournier."

The informer turned and saw the gun raised in the killer's hand. He snatched up the bag of tomatoes and money and started to run into the market. Kurt fired twice, the fat man stumbled and then fell heavily into a market stall, scattering the produce as the woman in charge of the stall screamed and stepped back.

Fournier was dead before he hit the ground. The bag containing the tomatoes and the money fell beside him. Calmet, who had been standing at one of the other stalls, walked forward briskly, bent down and took the money, putting it into his pocket as he walked quickly away into the crowd before anyone noticed him.

When Johnny presented himself at the yacht club at about a quarter to one that day, he was not wearing his guns. However, he had a coat folded over his arm and a pistol was in one pocket. He left the coat and pistol in the cloakroom and went through into the dining room as the receptionist told him that he was expected.

Lucienne was not alone—but accompanied by her Father and Madame Apcar. He felt a sudden prickling nervousness which he swept aside in his mind—there was no reason to be troubled. Why shouldn't Brizard come to the yacht club for lunch, there was nothing to stop him. He did, however, note with some amusement that Wilson was standing near the glass window, protection ever in evidence. Issuing forth for a social occasion was not going to lessen Brizard's instincts for self-preservation.

As he entered the room, Lucienne rose and came over to him:

"Hello, darling. I hope you don't mind my father. He decided to come at the last moment."

"Not at all. I feel safer with him here." He accompanied the weak sally with a leer and a wink and she kissed him again, a kiss that was full of promise.

He came over to the table, shook hands gravely with Brizard and kissed Madame Apcar's hand, a gesture which produced no expression on Brizard's face, but a fluttering of feminine eyelashes and smiles from the recipient and a physical stiffening of tension in Lucienne. Obviously the sexual jealousy of daughter for mistress lurked very close to the surface of their apparently friendly relationship.

As at dinner the night before, Jacques Brizard dominated the conversation from the start of the meal. He was used to dominating any situation in which he found himself and did it easily, even if he was a little pompous for Johnny's taste.

During the main course, he asked suddenly:

"Do you like boxing, Mr. Davos?"

"Please call me Johnny."

"I'm sorry, Johnny. But that does not answer my question."

Johnny thought for a moment, trying for the sort of answer that he judged the other man would appreciate:

"Well," he said at last. "Not often. The fighters don't seem to have the magic that one has heard of the older generation."

His answer was as pompous as the other man's usual declamations and he responded accordingly, warming to his guest:

"That's my opinion too. You know why?"

"Not really."

Again Brizard beamed, able to hold forth with yet another of his own opinions. He was used to having his opinions over-ride others:

"The killer instinct has gone. Today boxing is nothing other than big business. Fighters are no longer hungry."

Lucienne sighed:

"Really, Father, boxing is so boring, couldn't we talk about something else."

Brizard glanced triumphantly round him, a point scored:

"You see what I mean, Mr. Davos—Johnny. Today, boxing is indeed boring. But my father could have been middle-weight champion of the world. In the end it wasn't a question of strength or speed—it was the question of a woman."

Madame Apcar giggled tactlessly, as usual:

"Like father, like son."

Brizard coloured angrily and glared at her, but she was saved a cutting rejoinder as the maitre d'hotel of the establishment came forward:

"Pardon me, Monsieur, you are wanted on the telephone."

As he bowed and walked away, Brizard rose:

"Excuse me."

He wiped his lips on his napkin and left it on the table. He walked quickly across the room and disappeared into the entrance hall of the club. He picked up the phone that was waiting for him in one of the booths:

"Yes."

"Calmet—can you speak."

"Go ahead."

"I have some information on John Davos."

Brizard was at once alert, he glanced round to make sure that he was not going to be overheard:

"Well, man?"

"Davos's real name is Deray. He's wanted by the Paris police on warrants for robbery and murder."

"Are you certain."

There was a short pause, then Calmet said firmly:

"Yes, I'm absolutely certain."

"Where are you?"

"Near the new building."

"Alone?"

"No. Minieri is here, remember. We have to pay him for the job he did for us in Paris on Ventura—the information, remember?"

"Right. I'll be right there. Wait for me. Davos or

Deray or whatever his name is could be useful to us in this matter, at any rate."

He broke the connection and walked briskly back into the restaurant:

"You must excuse me, ladies. Something has come up. Business."

He turned elaborately away, then back to Johnny:

"I've an idea. Would you care to take a ride with me? There's some things I'd like to talk to you about on the way. We'll be back with the ladies in time for coffee."

Johnny glanced surreptitiously at Lucienne, who smiled and nodded almost imperceptibly. She was very pleased. Her Father never reacted this way to her young men.

"Excuse me." Johnny rose and walked out of the dining room with Brizard. Lucienne stared at the back of this man she wanted so badly and Madame Apcar had to wave her hand in front of the girl's face to get her attention back to the table.

In the hall, as Wilson stood close to Brizard, Johnny made for the cloakroom:

"Excuse me. I won't be a moment."

Before either of the men could follow, he had slipped into the cloakroom and asked for his coat. He slipped the gun from it and into his inside pocket and was returning the coat as Wilson joined him in the cloakroom.

The three men walked briskly out to the street, where the chauffeur was waiting at the wheel of Brizard's sleek, custom-built Rolls-Royce. For a criminal, thought Johnny, Brizard certainly knew how to live.

He and Johnny climbed in the back and Wilson sat in the passenger seat in the front. Brizard pressed a button and the glass window between the two halves of the car rolled down. Then he reached forward and switched on the radio, turning the dial to a station that was playing classical music, before he said:

"The new building."

The car moved off smoothly. It was like driving on a rubber cushion. Brizard was silent for only a short time, then:

"Most of us are creatures of habit."

Johnny did not respond and he went on:

"Don't you agree."

"For most of the time, yes."

"Oh come now, for more than you'd perhaps admit at first thought. We all stay with the same products—we drive the same cars—we tend to eat the same food."

Johnny nodded. He couldn't see where the conversation was leading, but sensed a sudden danger in it:

"We all fall into a pattern—I'll agree that."

Brizard smiled:

"Yes. Now take me, I've been to the same tailor for thirty years. When I am comfortable with certain things I stay with them."

"So do I."

He found it a little off-putting that the driver and Wilson were both very obviously observing him in the rear-view mirror and he hoped that the driver at least had half an eye on the busy road.

Brizard's next remark brought all his faculties up sharp like a douche of cold water:

"In your case, I am sure that you always use the same kind of gun."

He glanced at Brizard, but the man's face was bland, there was no challenge on it, only curiosity. Johnny wondered how much the man had guessed, how much he had discovered. Still, there was nothing to be lost now by being less than honest:

"Well, that depends on the job."

Brizard nodded, his face and voice still controlled and pleasant. He might have been asking what the other man usually ate for breakfast:

"What kind are you carrying now, for instance?"

Johnny did not hesitate, but reached inside his coat and produced his pistol, butt first, so as to obviate the necessity for Wilson making any mistakes as to his intentions. Inside, he felt queasy, on the surface he had lost none of his urbane calm.

Brizard took the gun from him, inspected it and weighed it in his palm. Wilson turned round and Brizard handed the gun to the man who did the same as his master, then handed it back:

"I admire your choice. It is a useful little weapon."

To Johnny's stunned surprise, the gun was back in his hand and he was controlling the desire to shake for long enough to return it to his inside pocket without fumbling.

The journey continued in silence as the huge car turned off the main road onto a building site, then halted by a pile of construction materials, including a huge mountain of shale, used for mixing ferro-concrete.

Wilson and the driver jumped out as the car stopped and each opened one of the rear doors for Brizard and Johnny to climb down. As he came round the front of the car to join his host, Brizard looked up and Johnny's eyes followed his. The construction was of a tall skyscraper. From where he stood, almost directly beneath it, it looked to Johnny as if some twenty-five stories of the shell had been put up. The interior of the building was still a cavern of struts, with concrete divisions between the floors. The means of getting up it seemed to be a temporary lift which consisted of a wire cage on the outside of the building. Brizard said:

"I have to see the foreman. Come with me."

The two men climbed into the lift and Brizard shut the gates, leaving Wilson and the driver on the ground. Johnny glanced round. Even if he could evade Wilson and the other man afterwards, this was not a good place to do his job. The cage was completely enclosed, there was no way to push Brizard out.

As the lift started up the side of the building, Brizard turned to him with his bland smile:

"I hope you're not afraid of heights."

Johnny smiled. He was counting the floors as they went past and quickly became aware that he had underestimated the height of the building, it was nearer to thirty-five stories:

"Not at all."

Brizard was silent for a moment, then, when he spoke again, his blandness was gone, his voice was harsh:

"Why have you lied to me?"

"Lied?"

Every nerve in Johnny's body was tingling, but he kept his outward control with some difficulty. But Brizard's next words shook his equanimity more than ever, and left him completely confused and bewildered—out on a limb that had not been of his devising:

"The police are looking for you."

"The police?"

"Yes, for bank robbery and murder."

Johnny took a deep breath as he tried to work out what had happened. There was no explanation that seemed reasonable at that moment:

"I don't rob banks. That's not my line."

"What is your line?"

Then he didn't know. Johnny felt the tension ease slightly and he was more confident in his next reply:

"That depends on what you want done."

Brizard spoke slowly, much as a normal person might ask for a light for his cigarette:

"I want you to kill somebody."

The irony of the situation was not lost on the professional killer. Well, every job had its little twists, though this one was becoming alarmingly labyrinthine:

"How much will you pay?"

"Fifty thousand dollars."

Now Johnny was worried again. The sum of money was the same as he had been paid to kill Brizard. The man must know. He kept his voice level:

"When?"

"Now."

Johnny nodded, maintaining his outward calm. Inside, his mind was racing as he tried to piece together a set of circumstances that would explain how he had come to be known by Brizard as a murderer and bank robber. The only conclusion which was impossible to dismiss was that the foul-up had occurred through some collusion between Steve Ventura and Inspector Briac of the Sureté—or perhaps through Briac playing some game of his own.

He had always made it a rule never to trust the police of any country and, when Briac had made the original contact with him about a job, it had been his first instinct to refuse even to discuss it, to even deny that he understood what the policeman might be talking about when he referred to a 'job'.

He had only taken interest in the policeman's call when the man had mentioned that his employer would be Steve Ventura. Steve he remembered and liked. He had always been able to trust him, knowing that the American would sooner die than betray a friend. He was rather surprised that Steve should want such a job done—he was the sort of man who would do such a killing himself—or would work within the law to eliminate somebody, a man of conscience. So Johnny had known that Steve must be in bad trouble to want such a thing done, to be prepared to hire a killer to do the job for him.

No, it could not be Steve—unless. And here his mind paused for a moment as he realised that his present difficult position could have been brought about by Steve Ventura's conscience. Perhaps the man had got cold feet and had asked Briac to take Johnny out of circulation so as to be able to contact him to cancel the contract—or, perhaps Steve had some way to get Brizard, though the killer considered this unlikely.

Anyway, such speculation was idle at the moment, time to sort out what had happened later—that is if he survived the next few minutes. And, as the lift cage came to the thirty-fifth and final floor of the building, Johnny Deray felt as close to death as he had done in a long time. He managed a smile for the watching Brizard and said:

"I think you misunderstood the question. I meant when do I get the fifty thousand dollars."

"Now." repeated Brizard, sliding back the door of the lift cage and stepping out on to the half-completed roof of the tall building. Johnny followed him, paused, and looked around.

The view very nearly took his breath away. All around the whole city of Marseilles was laid out in his view. To the north were the blue hills and green valleys of France and, to the south, beyond the dwarfed port, the matching blue of the sea. The building commanded the best view and was the tallest building in the city.

At the base of the building he had seen no sign of any workers and had at first assumed they were enjoying their lunch-time break, but now that he knew the reason for being brought there he speculated on how the workmen had been persuaded off the site and what would be the result of a violent death there when they returned later.

Closer to hand, the piece of roof on which he and Brizard were standing was firm; then there came a gap that only fell one floor and was bridged by twin planks. Beyond this was another firm area and on it stood two men. One was tall and thin, an Algerian in faded jeans and a tattered sweat shirt; the other man in a suit and light raincoat. Johnny recognised this second man at once. This was Calmet, Brizard's principal lieutenant. It therefore followed that the victim of the crime he was being invited to undertake was the other man—unless, with supreme irony, Brizard intended him to be the victim anyway.

As he was not supposed to know Calmet's identity, he turned to Brizard and pointed at the two men:

"Which one?"

Brizard replied:

"The tall one on the left."

"And the other man?"

Brizard laughed:

"He is too valuable to both of us. His name is Calmet. He's the one who's going to pay you."

He moved forward and, as Johnny followed suit, he snapped:

"No. Stop here a moment."

Johnny nodded and waited as Brizard crossed on one of the planks to the other side of the roof. He nodded to Calmet, then faced Minieri, the paid informer:

"I am Jacques Brizard."

The man was overawed to a pathetic degree, blushing and bowing his head at meeting such a big man. He seemed unable to speak for the moment and Brizard went on with a slight show of impatience:

"Calmet tells me that you've done a good job for us. I wanted to thank you personally and to make sure that you were properly paid for your troubles—are you content?"

"Oh, thank you, Mr. Brizard, thank you."

Brizard turned and pointed across the roof to Johnny—who was wondering what Brizard was saying and praying that it wasn't putting nails in his coffin—and said:

"He'll pay you when we have gone."

"Thank you, Sir."

Minieri bowed low and Brizard turned to go back to the lift, beckoning Calmet to follow him. The two men crossed back to where Johnny was standing, his face a picture of studied calm, his brain seething with unpalatable alternatives as he waited.

Calmet walked straight to the lift and opened the gate for his master. Brizard paused by Johnny for a second, nodded, flicked his eyes towards where Minieri was waiting, with no suspicion of his intended fate, then walked on and into the lift. The gates shut and the two men disappeared from sight leaving no sound other than the perpetual wind that always blew at such a height.

Johnny walked slowly forward and balanced himself carefully across the plank. He had already worked out the cleanest and most professional way to waste the Algerian, who was inviting death, standing with his back to the edge of the roof. It would be a relief not to use a gun, but, as he moved forward, he reached in his pocket and put his hand on the butt just in case.

Minieri smiled as he came close, revealing gaps in his teeth, the rest in an advanced state of decay. The irrelevant thought went through Johnny's mind that at least the poor man wouldn't have any further trouble with his teeth. He caught himself up, irritated at his own meanderings.

Minieri coughed ingratiatingly:

"Mr. Brizard said that you have my money."

His right hand still holding the butt of his gun in his inside jacket pocket, his left hand shot out and caught the doomed man full in the chest. Minieri gasped, teetered for a moment on the edge of the roof, then plunged down and out of Johnny's sight.

Listening to the scream of the man, Johnny felt a line of sweat form on his brow. Then there was a muffled thud and the noise ceased instantly. Johnny took his hand off the gun butt and was annoyed to feel that it was damp. He wiped his brow, turned and walked over to the lift.

As he pressed the button to call the cage up, his mind was working at whirlwind speed. He had no idea what to expect when he arrived on the ground level again. Perhaps Calmet had been told to dispose of him after he had done Brizard's killing for him. Still, that was a situation that he would have to face in a moment and he should utilise his time preparing for it.

He stepped to one side as the cage reached the roof, just in case there was anyone aboard. Seeing it empty, he smiled at his own fear, while still aware that it never did any harm to take full precautions. He got in and pressed the down button, transferring his gun into his outside jacket pocket.

Nearing the base of the building, he glanced down and saw that Calmet was waiting for him by the huge pile of shale which had acted as a cushion for the falling body of the doomed Algerian. The Rolls-Royce had disappeared and there was only one small car—presumably Calmet's—waiting near the entrance to the construction site. It would provide a good getaway if he had to fight it out with Calmet.

The cage reached the ground and Calmet came forward, opening the gates before Johnny had had time to move:

"Let me have your billfold."

Johnny hesitated for a moment, the unasked question on his face. Calmet frowned:

"Quickly, we haven't much time."

Johnny decided to trust the man. He handed him the billfold. Calmet flicked through it and nodded, satisfied, then:

"When the police find the body, your wallet will be in his pocket."

Johnny shook his head:

"It won't work. When they find him, they'll spot the difference straight away."

Calmet smiled. It was a grimace entirely without humour and Johnny felt a shiver down his spine as he saw it:

"Not when I'm done with him. You wait for me in the car and I will take you back to the yacht club when I've finished."

Johnny noticed for the first time that Calmet was wearing rubber surgical gloves, and he was only too happy to turn away and walk to the car as the man climbed up the shale, making hard work of it as it gave slightly under him, causing small avalanches to the base.

It took Calmet only ten minutes to do the work he had to do. As he walked over to the car, he was peeling off the now blood-stained gloves. He opened the driving door of the car, took a little plastic bag off the dashboard shelf and put the gloves into it before climbing in, starting the engine and driving off. In all this, Johnny saw no emotion on his face. The man was a real professional, no doubt of that, a worthy adversary as far as Johnny was concerned and he was relieved that the other man was apparently on his side.

They started the drive back to the yacht club in silence. Johnny tried to make conversation:

"Calmet? Do you have another name."

The driver shrugged:

"Everyone calls me Calmet, they always have. I am used to it. That is what you will call me in future."

"In future?" Johnny could not keep the surprise out of his voice.

Calmet looked at him sharply, the sunlight glinting off his thick spectacles:

"You are not happy at the idea of working for Mr. Brizard?"

"I didn't realise that I was. I thought it was a one-off job."

Calmet shook his head:

"Mr. Brizard was testing you. I will tell him that you passed his test. It was a good clean job, much as I would have done it myself. By the way, this is yours—the first instalment of what your new job will pay you."

He slipped one hand into his breast pocket and produced a bulky package similar to the one that Steve Ventura had given him in Paris when he had hired him for the assignment. He opened the envelope and began to count the neat stack of American currency that was crammed into it. Calmet gave him a sidelong glance:

"You trust nobody. That is a good thing in our profession. I think we will work well together."

Johnny laughed inwardly. Trust nobody, that was a good one. He could remember when he had stuffed Steve's envelope into his coat pocket, not counting it because he trusted him. And now look at the mess he was in. Somehow he couldn't quite believe that

Jacques Brizard had fallen for the robbery and murder line quite as hard as he appeared to. Either he knew who Johnny was, in which case he was on red alert from that moment on—or he had strung along with the image because there was a dirty job he wanted done, and he didn't want it to touch any of his own organisation. Whichever the answer was, it didn't look good for Johnny Deray.

He put the money back into the envelope and into his inside pocket as the car swept round the corner and came to a halt at the entrance to the yacht club. Johnny noted that the Rolls-Royce was once more parked conspicuously in front of the building. Calmet said:

"I will see you again soon. Mr. Brizard is expecting you for the end of luncheon."

Johnny nodded and walked up the steps, into the club and straight into the dining room. It was deserted now, but for Brizard's party. As he entered the room, Lucienne half-rose, then subsided back into her chair, obviously nervous, obviously worried for him. He went over and Brizard smiled up at him:

"Ah, John, here you are. I was just telling Madame Apcar and my daughter that you have decided to work for me."

Johnny inclined his head in agreement and walked back to his place. Lucienne's eyes were burning with worry, but he affected to ignore them. The party drank coffee in a restrained and polite silence after which Brizard glanced at his watch:

"We have to be getting back to the villa. I am expecting some calls." He turned particularly to Johnny. "Perhaps you would like to come with us. I understand you are taking my daughter out this evening and I don't see why she need be deprived of your company for the afternoon."

Johnny inclined his head:

"Lucienne?"

"Please come, Johnny."

"For you, I will." His eyes were fixed again on Lucienne's father, a challenge thrown to the older man. He said slowly: "I work for myself, Mr. Brizard. You have contracted my services."

The other man nodded:

"I had no wish to give the impression that my invitation to you for the afternoon was in any way in the nature of an order."

His voice was soft, but glancing at the faces of the two women and seeing the fear in their eyes, he realised that Jacques Brizard at his most urbane was also at his most dangerous.

CHAPTER NINE

For the second consecutive morning, Steve Ventura made his way to his office at the Embassy in a state of threatening depression. There had been no word from Inspector Briac on Johnny Deray, though he had assured the American that particular trouble had been taken with the Marseilles police to tell them in confidence that the man they were seeking for robbery and murder could be found somewhere in the vicinity of Jacques Brizard. Steve could only conclude that either Johnny had not yet started on his mission, or that the Marseilles police establishment was so afraid of Brizard that they didn't even dare get close enough to see who might be close to him.

He was wrapped up in these and similar thoughts when he entered his office, blinked, then focussed his eyes on the scene that greeted him, unable to comprehend it:

"What the hell?"

His desk was covered in a spotless white damask table cloth and at one side had been carefully placed a vase of open yellow tulips. On the other side, a bottle of red wine rested in a silver pouring cradle, two glasses of red wine poured out, ready and waiting. Sally, who had got up an hour early to get in to the office and accomplish these special effects, was seated in his swivel chair, its back to the door, staring out of the window. At the sound of his entry, she turned the chair to face him:

"Morning, chief."

Steve gagged for a moment, then managed:

"What the hell is this in aid of?"

Sally laughed:

"Well, you said you hated this desk, didn't you?"

Steve started to laugh, the tension of his worries draining out of him. He crossed to the couch at the side of the office and sat down heavily:

"That's very good, Sally, very funny."

He sat laughing for a minute, then his gloom overtook him afresh:

"What else is new?"

Sally handed him his glass of wine and he stared at it:

"Bit early in the day, honey. Anyway, it all tastes like Muscatel to me."

"Thank you kind sir. Anyhow, there's nothing much getting ready to blow up in your face this morning except Williams and the auditors are hot on your trail."

"No call from Inspector Briac?"

"Not a word—what's it about, perhaps I could help?"

Steve shook his head quickly:

"No. It's a private matter. He and I have a bet. I think the son-of-a-bitch is trying to welch."

Sally nodded. She didn't believe a word of it, but she knew better than to tell Steve he was a liar:

"What shall I do about the auditors."

"What do they want?"

"Well, for one thing, Williams says your department is twenty six percent over budget."

Steve lifted his glass in a silent toast and sipped:

"To hell with them."

Sally giggled:

"Secondly, they say its been weeks since you sent in your expense account."

Steve rose, irritated by this minor detail of routine that was part of the constant minutiae of his desk job, the job he had never wanted in the first place:

"Look, Sally, I'm a policeman. I expect you to be the bookkeeper, remember."

"Yes, Sir. Mind you, I quite agree with them."

"About what." He turned and glowered at her so that she shrank a little. She mumbled:

"Well, fifty thousand dollars is rather a lot of money."

"Listen, that's secret fund. I told you that I'll take care of that." He returned to the couch and sat down to finish his glass of wine. He smiled up at Sally, regretting his slap-down of a moment before. She responded as he knew she would, sidling over to him, taking the glass from his hand and sitting close to him on the couch:

"Steve, you can tell little Sally. What did you really do with all that money."

Playing along with her mockery, he took her in his arms and hugged her hard. It felt good and he realised he needed her very much at that lonely moment. Rita was gone and had not called him as he had expected, and now, with Johnny Deray hanging over his head like an unexploded bomb, he felt very vulnerable and more inwardly frightened than he had done since his days in the field. He managed a light answer:

"I've stashed it away in Switzerland, baby."

Sally laughed:

"Then why don't you and I take a nice long cruise?"
"That's not a bad idea, kid."

A moment later, they were locked in an embrace that was the real thing. With the superb timing that can only occur at such moments the telephone, which Sally had hidden under the desk, shrilled with an insistent ring. Sally pulled herself out of his arms:

"Damn."

Steve managed a light smile and tapped her playfully on her well-rounded rump. She wasn't a bad broad, not bad at all:

"Get to work, get to work."

She squatted down by the desk, her knees demurely together and picked up the phone:

"Hello, Mr. Ventura's office. Who's speaking please?" She listened for a moment, then cupped the mouthpiece:

"It's Inspector Briac."

Steve leapt off the couch and grabbed the phone unceremoniously from her:

"Briac?"

The Inspector's voice sounded worried:

"Can you talk?"

Ventura glanced round at Sally, who was watching him with puzzled interest. His anxiety was catching:

"Not at the moment."

"I must meet you," said Briac. "It's about Deray. I'll see you in the Raphael Bar in thirty minutes."

"Right." Steve slammed down the receiver and whirled on Sally: "I have to go out."

"Well, what about Fred Williams. When can I tell him you'll be back."

Steve snorted:

"You tell Fred Williams that I have a message for him and the first word is 'go'. Either he or his secretary will be able to fill in the rest."

She was left standing as he rushed out, the door slamming with an air of threatening finality behind him.

Briac was waiting for him at the entrance to the bar. The look of concern on his face mirrored his worried voice on the phone. Steve blundered past him and slipped into the first booth. Another sign of the Inspector's concern came as he failed to order a drink and slipped in opposite the American. He began without preamble:

"Deray is still in Marseilles."

Steve snapped:

"You picked him up?"

Briac shook his head:

"You could say that. He went off the top floor of a thirty-five storey building. He is in the morgue."

He waited as Steve Ventura's mouth fell open. For a moment he thought that the usually tough, uncompromising man who faced him was going to burst into tears. He said, more softly:

"Did you hear what I said? Deray is dead."

Steve nodded and said gruffly:

"Thanks, I heard."

Both men were silent for a moment, each for their own reasons. Steve felt an overwhelming desire to break something in his rage and frustration. He had given in to temptation, had sought the easy way out and it had cost the death of an old friend, a friend who had, on more than one occasion in those long gone days in the Congo, saved his life.

Briac waited for Steve to look more receptive and at last the American said, in a voice that showed evidence of his effort to speak calmly:

"Have you any idea what happened?"

Briac shrugged:

"None at all. The only information is that the construction company that worked on the building belongs to Jacques Brizard."

"When did it happen?"

"Sometime yesterday. Some essential materials had not arrived and the men were off the site for a long break. When they came back the body was there. It was horribly mutilated, falling thirty-five floors face down on a pile of shale. If it hadn't been for his bill fold, we would never have got the identification."

Steve rose abruptly:

"Thanks."

He walked straight out of the bar and back to the Embassy, not pausing to look left or right as he crossed the road. Inside, he walked straight into his office. Sally, who had been setting his desk back to rights turned with a cheerful smile:

"What about our cruise?" The smile died on her lips as she saw his pale face and clenched fists. He walked past her and snatched up his briefcase:

"The joke's over. Get me a ticket to Marseilles."

On the surface, Johnny showed no sign of his inward fears as in the wake of Brizard's Rolls he entered the opened gates of the villa in his car. He followed it up the drive to the front of the villa, and the Alfa glided to a halt outside the entrance, just behind the other car. He saw Lucienne jump out and come running over to him. He switched off the engine and stepped out and she said:

"What is this about you working for my father? He would not speak about it in the car."

Johnny shrugged:

"I wasn't satisfied with what I was getting in the firm I'm with. Your father gave me a better offer, that's all there is to it."

She was not to be side-tracked so easily:

"But what are you going to do for him?"

"I don't know yet, but he seems to want me."

They walked together up the steps and into the villa. Lucienne was about to press her question when Johnny pointed up to the camera in the hall and put his finger to his lips in a gesture of silence:

"Later, huh."

She reddened angrily, shook off his arm and ran up the stairs, while he watched her go. When she was at the top, he called:

"We'll go out this evening. Talk then."

She looked down, a sudden flashing smile which told him all he needed to know of what she would want from him:

"Alright—after dinner." Then she was out of sight.

Johnny glanced round. The hallway was deserted, Brizard and Madame Apcar having preceded himself and Lucienne into the villa, and he felt hot and sticky, a reaction to the work he had done earlier in the day, and the precarious position he now found himself in. On the one hand, it was nice to know that the police wouldn't be looking for him any longer on the robbery and murder charge that had been concocted—on the other hand, he was now completely at the mercy of Jacques Brizard and his people—and Brizard had placed him in that position for a special reason, he had no illusions on that score.

He spotted the door to the hall washroom and made for it, stripping off his coat, which was weighing him down with its load of a gun and the extra fifty thousand dollars he had earned himself over lunch.

He want inside and admired the fittings in the washroom—all brown leather and art nouveau. He found a peg at the far end, hung up his jacket and was about to turn on one of the ostentatious gold taps at a marble washstand when he heard Brizard's voice:

"Hello . . . Yes, it was arranged . . . No, he should not know till tomorrow. . . ."

The man was obviously talking on the phone to somebody and the voice came from the end of the washroom, where he had hung his coat. Johnny tiptoed forward to investigate and noticed the crack where an apparently solid wall was in fact a concealed door—a door that, from what he knew of the lay-out to the villa, must enter Brizard's study behind one of the book-cases. It was slightly ajar and Johnny did not disturb it further as he put his ear to the crack. There was a pause, then Brizard said, with a tone of patience in his voice:

"Yes, but I believe he may prove useful. I would, however, like to know a little more about him."

There was another pause, then:

"No, I'm not asking for your opinion, just facts . . ."

Another long silence:

"Put it this way. I am formally requesting information in regard to a new employee."

A shorter pause this time:

"Good. It is Davos, D . . . A . . . V . . . O . . . S . . ., like the town in Switzerland. I will wait to hear from you."

The receiver was replaced and Johnny hurriedly backed from the door, taking his jacket, and abandoning the idea of washing his hands for the moment. He was walking up the hallway when Brizard appeared in his study doorway:

"Ah, Mr. Davos. Have you seen my daughter? I think she was with you."

Johnny pointed upwards:

"I think she went to her room."

Brizard nodded his thanks and began to climb the stairs. He was about half-way up when Johnny said:

"Excuse me?"

"Yes?"

"Have you anywhere where I could wash my hands. I'm feeling a little sticky after the drive."

He spent the afternoon marking time on the lawn of the villa with Madame Apcar, steering the conversation continually away from the personal and back into the general as much as he could. Brizard's mistress seemed anxious to signal to him that she was available —and Johnny might have felt tempted to put her apparent eagerness to the test under other circumstances —but, now was not the time.

If Jacques Brizard had no compunction about wasting an employee to provide a cover for a new man, then he would certainly not give his whole-hearted approval to his mistress taking an extra lover from amongst the newly-hired help. In addition, they were never out of sight or earshot of the ubiquitous Wilson, who doubtless would report Johnny's every utterance to his employer at the first available opportunity.

Of Lucienne there was no sign, but Johnny assumed that she was staying in sulky dignity in her room, though he had hopes that she was going to get over her attack of pique at his new employment by that evening.

Dinner was served early on the terrace and as Brizard glanced round at the other three diners, he seemed relaxed and at ease. Lucienne appeared last, wearing a severely-cut black evening dress that accentuated the promise of her young figure and she favoured Johnny with a dazzling smile that relieved his fears with regard to the evening's entertainment. Tonight was to be the night. His orderly soul told him that it was rushing things a bit, but it had always been his experience that the rich are less patient than ordinary mortals.

He was also amused to note that the dazzling smile had not escaped the attention of Madame Apcar who shot her lover's daughter a malevolent glance when his back was turned as Lucienne leant over to kiss her father on the forehead.

As the meal was served, Brizard, who seemed in a particularly avuncular frame of mind, beamed on the assembled company:

"I have asked the chef to serve us something light as the young people are intending to go into town for the evening."

Johnny, who was feeling particularly old after a sorely-trying day, bridled inwardly at his description as a 'young person', but smiled dutifully in turn with the other insincere reactions to Brizard's sally.

During the body of the meal there was little conversation beyond a desultory exchange about the guest list for the charity dinner and ball on the eighteenth of the month. The occasion was now little more than a week away and Madame Apcar, who had been entrusted with the guest list, was still struggling with it.

Brizard seemed amused by her fear that she was causing him displeasure by her delay, but Johnny noticed that there were good reasons for her fluttering excuses. Underneath his avuncular exterior of good humour, Jacques Brizard was as ruthless in his personal relationships as he was in his business dealings, both legal and illegal, and Madame Apcar had probably good reason to know of his displeasure and its results. To be owned by such a man must at some times have been less of a bed of roses than it appeared on the surface.

Lucienne did her best to intervene on the other woman's behalf with an offer of assistance but her father glared at her:

"No, my dear. Let her do it on her own. It is little enough I ask of her, isn't it?" This last was directed at the hapless Madame Apcar herself, who lowered her eyes and said in a voice that was little more than a whisper:

"Yes, Jacques. I'm sorry."

Johnny thought it was about time the uncomfortable little party broke up and he signalled Lucienne with a nod of his head. She took her cue and rose from her chair:

"Father, I think we should be going."

Johnny prepared to rise as Brizard smiled and got up to kiss his daughter. He turned to Johnny:

"For the rest of your stay in Marseilles you must be our guest here at the villa. When you come back tonight, please bring your bags. I will have the guest room prepared."

This was the last thing Johnny wanted:

"That's most kind, but I wouldn't put you to any trouble."

Brizard's eyes glinted, showing that it was an order, not a request:

"It won't be any trouble at all. We enjoy having guests, don't we my dear?"

This last was addressed to Madame Apcar, who still had her eyes down on her plate. She looked up now, hoping that the tone of his voice showed that she had been forgiven for her omissions in regard to the Charity guest lists and fluttered her eye-lashes:

"Yes, Jacques, of course."

He beamed at her, but there was not an ounce of warmth in the smile. Madame Apcar was obviously in for a stormy evening, thought Johnny.

He followed Lucienne from the terrace back into the villa. She paused just inside the french windows for him to catch up so that she could take his hand, pressing herself against him as she did so. He accepted the pressure of her body with a look of amused stoicism which caught the right note in her and made her giggle as she stepped away. They walked in silence to the front door and Johnny paused while she collected a wrap.

Outside, on the steps, she said:

"Let's go in my car."

He held up his hands in mock alarm:

"Over my dead body. Which it probably would be, the way you drive."

She made a mock feint at him and he ducked away and ran down the steps to the door of his own car. Lucienne shrugged:

"What must be, must be."

When they reached the gates of the villa, Johnny noticed that the gate-keeper checked on the phone inside his little office before opening the gates. So Brizard kept as watchful an eye on his daughter's safety as he did his own. That, at least, was a point in his favour.

On the drive into town, Lucienne was silent and relaxed, showing her intentions only by the pressure of her hand on his knee as they took the bends at an intoxicating speed. As they entered the town, Johnny said:

"Where shall we go?"

"The yacht club. Where else?"

Johnny tried to argue:

"But if we're not with your father and his damned television cameras, we're at the yacht club—and doubtless he gets a report from the management as to how his little girl is behaving."

She nodded:

"If you must know, he owns the place. And, yes, he does get reports."

"Why the hell do you put up with it?"

She shrugged:

"My father is a very powerful man in the community. He has many enemies, once, two years ago . . ." Her voice faded away as the car came to a halt. She reached for the door handle, but he grasped her arm, holding her back:

"Tell me." His voice was quiet, but compelling.

She sighed:

"There was some trouble about a construction contract for the City. Some men tried to kidnap me. I don't like to remember it. Mr. Calmet shot one of them and there was a lot of trouble. Since then, I have done what my Father says. He had always warned me that my life might be in danger, but I had never believed him until then."

From the tone of her voice, Johnny realised that she had no knowledge of her Father's real activities, but truly believed that it was a business deal that had been the cause of the attempt on her.

Out loud, he smiled:

"And what about young men—or not so young men?"

She smiled back at him, her eyes suddenly dancing with pleasure as the old memory faded:

"They are all carefully checked out and he tells me which ones are alright and which are not."

"Charming."

She assumed an expression of amuzed coquetry:

"Do you want to know what he told me about you this afternoon?"

"I don't think I do," laughed Johnny. "I'm a modest sort at heart."

"I'll tell you anyway. He said you reminded him of him when he was your age, and that he couldn't give a higher recommendation than that. Mind you, he did warn me that I was in danger of being swept off my feet and out of my depth by you—am I out of my depth?"

He leant across and kissed her hard on the mouth. She responded to him with an intensity that took his breath away. Obviously, there weren't many young men of whom Jacques Brizard approved—or perhaps not enough with the dauntless courage needed to face such a man if one was chasing his daughter. When they broke for air, he said:

"No, I somehow think that the water I play in is a little shallower than that. Come on, I'll take you inside before I drown."

He made to get out of the car, but she held him back:

"I want you now."

"Later," he said. "When we get back."

She sat back and pouted with annoyance, obviously unused to not having her own way:

"But the cameras? There is one in every room."

He laughed as he opened the door and climbed out:

"You promise to hang on till then and I'll show you how to deal with a small problem like that."

He helped her out of the car and they walked to the entrance of the club. On the threshold, he glanced at his watch:

"Tell you what, it's early yet. Why don't you go on inside and I'll join you in a little while."

"Why, what is it?"

He smiled reassuringly:

"Listen, I'd better go and get my stuff from the hotel, if I'm staying at the Villa. It won't take me a moment."

"I'll come with you. We can use the bed until you vacate the room, can't we?"

"I told you, love, save it for later. Anyway, I don't want to compromise you." He pointed back down the road. A car was parked there, its sidelights on—the car that had picked them up just outside the gates of the Villa and which contained Wilson, if Johnny was guessing aright.

"I understand," she said, kissing him gently on the cheek. "Don't be too long, or I might get bored."

He walked back to the car as she went inside. Climbing in, he roared off with his lights still out, did not flick the switch until he was out of sight of the other car, hoping that the suddenness of the manoeuvre had been enough to throw the other driver off as he turned sharply into an alley and wove through a series of back streets—to the hotel only two blocks away from the yacht club. He stopped the car in the side street and went round the front and into the hotel.

At the desk, he asked for the bill. Once upstairs he packed all but one of his cases. This last one he filled with the broken down pieces of his automatic rifle with the latest telescopic sights and the thick file that Steve Ventura had given him on the activities and associates of Jacques Brizard.

When the old man who acted as porter for the tiny establishment came to take the bags, this one he carried down himself, going ahead of the old man who was still wheezing down in the lift with the rest of the baggage.

The boot looked the same as that on any Alfa Romeo. Johnny felt for a lever on the left hand side, pushed it away from him and the section holding the spare wheel came loose and lifted up like a second boot lid. Inside were plastic bags containing two unlicensed and unregistered guns. He slipped the case with them, laying it carefully flat and replaced the false lid as the old man came wheezing up.

Johnny watched while he put the bags in the boot, then closed and locked it, not a moment too soon, as the car that had followed him from the villa came cruising along the street, obviously on a look-out for the Alfa. As it came to a halt, Johnny sauntered over. He had been wrong about the driver, he recognised Kurt from his picture in the file:

"Just collecting me bags, old son, no need to worry."

Kurt glared at him and said nothing and Johnny sauntered back to the hotel, paid his bill, came outside, got in the car and once more drove off, at a speed which his tail could not possibly match.

Arriving back at the yacht club, he parked the Alfa amid the mass of other cars in the car park instead of at the front and then waited on the step for his tail to arrive. As Kurt and the car passed the entrance, he gave a cheery wave and turned to go inside.

As he viewed the restaurant he thought that perhaps Lucienne's choice was not such a bad one after all. In contrast to the quietness during the day, the joint really jumped at night. There was a band, a girl singer and a large dance floor, which was provided by the removal of some of the tables that were over it at lunch-time. A bar dominated one end of the room, a running buffet the other. The night was mild so the great glass doors of the terrace had been slid back. In the midst of all this, some two hundred people, well-dressed, but most of them under thirty, were dancing and drinking.

He saw Lucienne signal him from the bar, where she was perched on a high stool, her small gold evening bag reserving the one next to her. He pushed his way through the throng and presented himself at her side:

"There, that didn't take too long, did it?"

She laughed:

"Only long enough for father to ring and ask where you'd gone and whether we'd had a row and I wanted picking up. He sounded hopeful, perhaps he didn't tell me the whole truth this afternoon?"

Johnny shouted his order for a Scotch to the barman, after noting that Lucienne was already equipped with a large vodka, before replying:

"I hope you disappointed him?"

"Of course," she smiled. "I trust you."

"And if you don't—and he doesn't trust you—well his pet goon followed me to check up."

His drink arrived and he took a swig, before asking her to dance. She accepted eagerly and, on the floor, she went wild to the music with the gay abandon of an animal, as if she was losing herself in it, free from the golden cage in which her father kept her, enveloped by the noise and the beat, far away from any earthly danger. Johnny found, in his clinically-detached mind, that he was feeling almost sorry for her, but put the thought firmly aside, aware that this was the first manifestation of weakness—and if it wasn't stamped upon quickly it could cost him his life.

She was a glutton for punishment and they were on the floor for a good thirty minutes before the band changed from the frenetic afro beats of the young to the slower, mooch music of a bygone era, Johnny's era. Then she clung to him, her hand stroking the fine blond hair at the back of his neck, her lips on his cheek as he smelt the fragrant promise of her perfume and felt her supple young body against his, pressing and rubbing against him. At last, he said:

"Steady, love, or you'll make an exhibition of both of us."

He led her off the dance floor and back to the bar, which was a great deal clearer than it had been earlier. They sat down at the end nearest the wall and ordered a round of drinks, watching each other quietly in the dim lights. The singer went into a mood number which fitted the moment as the drinks were brought to them and the barman discreetly retired. They clinked glasses, drank, then Lucienne put her hand on his thigh and asked the question he had been waiting for all evening:

"What sort of work are you going to do for my father?"

He shrugged:

"I haven't got the details yet. I expect the same sort of thing I've been doing up till now—trouble-shooting, that sort of thing." His face was deadpan, without a trace of a smile as he gave such an innocent explanation of his peculiar profession.

"Do you think you'll like working for him?"

"Why not? The money's good and the fringe benefits are great." He leant forward and kissed her lightly on the cheek. She responded, moving her mouth towards his, opened to him. After a moment, he was able to continue:

"Now let me ask you a question. With all you've told me, how do you like being your father's daughter?"

"I love it."

He laughed:

"All of it, or anything in particular?"

She responded in kind:

"The money's good and right now the fringe benefits are marvellous." Then, unexpectedly: "Is your father still alive?"

He was taken aback for a moment and could only reply with a flat: "No."

Lucienne sighed:

"Do you miss him?"

Johnny found that he was having to stop and think. His memory of his father was dim—an old man, his face worn to a leathery brown by the African sun, sitting on the verandah of his house, all the sounds of the African veldt round him, drinking beer from a can and swearing profusely at the white bastards who were giving the country away. Johnny had left to go about fighting for his land in his own way and one day he had received a letter to say that his father had been found in bed one morning, his throat cut from ear to ear, his number one boy from the farm missing. By the time he had received the letter, the funeral had taken place and it was too late even to mourn him. So he had got on with the job, with a degree more ruthlessness and a degree less mercy and discrimination between the various categories of his enemies, the intellectual, the guerrilla and the native.

He was recalled to the present by Lucienne hitting him on the knee:

"Penny for them."

"What?"

"I asked you if you missed your father and you wandered off into a dream. Is that yes or no?"

Johnny frowned:

"I used to miss him when he was alive but once I knew he was dead, I found that I didn't even really remember him."

"When did he die?"

He shrugged off the question:

"Oh, it was Africa, the time of the Congo break-up. It's ancient history."

Lucienne was more perceptive than he had given her credit for, as her next question proved:

"Are you afraid of dying?"

"I never think about it," he sighed. "Why bother about something that's bound to happen."

She sat up in surprise:

"But everybody thinks about it at some time."

"Well, they shouldn't until they come to it. That's the trouble with most people nowadays. They do too much thinking and too little doing."

"For example?"

Johnny squinted into his glass as he thought out his example. He was trying to remember what someone had once told him. He grinned as it came to him:

"A photographer once explained to me the difference between an amateur and a professional—He said an amateur thinks first and the moment's gone—the professional takes the moment and thinks about it afterwards."

Lucienne leant closer:

"Which are you?"

Johnny sipped his drink in silence. When he looked up, he was grinning mischievously, a twinkle in the normally cold blue eyes:

"Let me put it this way. If we should have such a moment, I would suggest that we take it and think about it afterwards."

They kissed, lingering passion welding them together. As they broke, Lucienne said:

"I can feel the moment."

They walked together out of the club, to Johnny's car and thus back to the villa. Johnny drove at a level cruising pace and in silence, Lucienne clinging to his shoulder, her tongue nuzzling his neck and ear. With one eye on the driving mirror, Johnny could see that Kurt was patiently on their tail. He felt irritated, was tempted to stop the car and give the thug a demonstration of his sexual technique at the side of the road. With anyone else besides Lucienne, perhaps he would have taken that course of action, but he found, in spite of his cool detachment about her as a piece of the jigsaw that was the job in hand, his feelings were also tender and protective towards her. He was falling into the very trap of weakness that he feared.

The car was allowed in with only one glance and Johnny was satisfied to see that the gates were closed immediately behind him, obviously a signal to Kurt that his services were no longer required now that Johnny and Lucienne were back in the grounds. He drove slowly to the villa, letting the car glide to a halt with the engine switched off. Lucienne was all over him and he gently untangled himself from her, got out of the car and helped her out and back into his arms. They returned from a long, cool kiss and she whispered:

"Your room or mine?"

"Mine," replied Johnny, also in a whisper. "If we can find out where it is."

They took his two cases and tiptoed up the steps. At the top, she told him to stop and wait for her:

"Why?"

"Alarm beams, switched on at night. I have a master key in my bag."

She went to the wall at the top of the steps, fumbled in the bag for a moment, found the key, opened a little box on the wall, cleverly hidden by a creeping plant, and inserted the key, turning it three times to the right. The professional in Johnny noted this in almost total darkness without thinking. He was pleased that he had judged a night assault on the villa as a wrong method of getting at Brizard—doubly glad he had picked Brizard's daughter as the route.

She was at his side again and led him into the villa. Inside, she closed the door quietly and turned a knob set into the wall:

"That reactivates the beams."

They went upstairs in the gloom of a single light burning down the hallway. There was a light burning in the upstairs corridor as well and Johnny allowed himself to be led down it as Lucienne pointed out her Father's room at the head of the stairs, then Madame Apcar's room, then her own. Johnny's guest room faced hers and she slipped inside with him and shut the door.

He snapped on the light. Jacques Brizard certainly did well by his special guests. He was confronted by a huge double bed, with giant size furniture of tables, chairs, drawers and wardrobe to match. It was the room's other contents that impressed him the most, however. A fully stocked cocktail cabinet winked its glass at him from the far side of the room

Lucienne caught hold of him and dragged him towards the bed. He stopped her and pointed up at the lens of the television camera, placed as usual where it could survey the whole room. She pulled away from him:

"You said you could deal with it."

He grinned:

"What are you wearing besides that dress?"

For an answer, she bent with a sudden movement and pulled the dress over her head. She stood before him in nothing barring a pair of sheer tights, her arms held, like a supplicant, at her sides. He eyed her critically:

"I'll have the tights, please."

Her face devoid of expression, she slipped them off and padded over to him, naked. He took the tights from her, pulled a chair over to the corner and climbed up in it, draping the tights over the camera. She laughed:

"But they're transparent. You can see through them."

Johnny nodded as he climbed down:

"Yes, love, but only a matted blur. You see they let in enough light for the screen to function as if there was interference, not enough to see a clear picture by—but, more importantly, not badly enough to signal a breakdown. You wouldn't like it if the TV repair men walked in during, would you?"

She walked to him and began to slip off his jacket:

"Wait a minute, love. I'm shy."

She lay on the bed, waiting with a cool patience as he undressed and then came to join her. In a few moments they were in each other's arms and she feasted from him with an abandoned urgency that was in direct contrast to the repression she must unconsciously live under, when one remembered the circumstances of car and siege under which her Father kept her.

Towards the end Johnny, for all his expertise, began to feel that he had met his match. But at last she curled into his side, warm and satisfied as they held each other close to sleep.

She whispered:

"I know what you are."

"What?"

"A professional." Then she was asleep in his arms.

Johnny Deray lay awake for a long time, feeling the gentle rise and fall of her breasts against his chest as she slept. For the first time in his life he felt ashamed of what he was doing, dirty and disgusted. He wanted to pack the whole thing in there and then, but there were two reasons he could not. First, his life now depended on keeping up the deception and, to his mind the more important reason, he had taken a contract, a contract from a friend.

Downstairs, in his study, Jacques Brizard read the report in front of him and then frantically twiddled the knob on the TV camera in the guest room, trying to get the small black and white picture into focus, unable to see whether there were one or two people in Johnny Davos's bed.

CHAPTER TEN

When Johnny woke on the morning following his night with Lucienne, she was gone from his bed. It was the manner of her going that brought about the process of his waking, for he could still feel the warmth of her against his back and on the bed next to him as he turned to survey the room. He looked up and grinned as he saw that her tights still obscured the television camera in the corner of the ceiling. He lay for a moment, luxuriating in the warmth of the bed, before being startled by an insistent knocking on his door. He called out:

"Just a minute."

Jumping from the covers, he was half-way across the room before he realised he was naked. He grabbed his topcoat from the chair where it had been thrown the evening before, before moving the same chair across the room, climbing up on it, removing the tights and stuffing them in his pocket. He opened the door.

Calmet stood in the corridor, his face its usual expressionless mask, his eyes glinting behind the thick glasses:

"Davos, Monsieur Brizard would like to see you

downstairs as soon as you are dressed." The information was given almost as an order, but not entirely, for Johnny could still sense a deference in the man as if he was not sure whether Johnny should be treated as an employee or a guest. Johnny smiled:

"Just give me ten minutes, love—oh, and a large pot of black coffee."

The other man's voice was still hard, though Johnny thought he could detect the trace of a smile playing round the corners of the man's mouth:

"You may have the ten minutes." He turned and walked briskly back down the corridor to the stairs, Johnny, staring after him, was suddenly apprehensive and on his guard.

He dressed and shaved quickly and within the ten minutes was descending the stairs in his shirt sleeves, his mouth a little thick from lack of coffee, but otherwise presentable.

Calmet was waiting for him at the bottom of the stairs and turned without speaking, beckoning Johnny to follow. He led him into the study, where Brizard was seated behind the desk, obviously waiting for him, for he rose as Calmet shut the door on the three of them. Johnny felt a certain degree of inner amusement battling with his nervousness as he saw that Brizard looked a little grey round the gills, as if he had been up very late, perhaps battling with the controls on a TV set rather than in the gentle arms of Madame Apcar.

He noticed a tray with a pot of coffee and three cups on a side table and crossed straight over to it. As he picked up the pot, Brizard said blandly:

"I was going to offer you a cup, but I see you've spotted it already. Both of us take black, Calmet, without sugar, but I prefer one spoonful. Then you may have yours and we can get down to a little business."

There was an edge of hardness behind the bland utterance and Johnny was aware that his host was subtly changing gear on their relationship—from guest to employee in three easy moves—and that this was the first chance to spot the mailed fist hidden in the velvet glove of Brizard's charm. Well, it would do no harm to show he knew his place, at least it meant that he was being accepted into the organisation.

He poured the coffee as directed and handed a cup to each of the men before returning to prepare his own—black with no sugar. He walked over to his desk with the cup and waited while Brizard spread out a map. It was upside down to him but a feature across the middle of it made it look like a chart for a section of the Great Wall of China.

"I have a little job for you. Come round here, you too Calmet."

Johnny and Calmet shuffled round the edge of the huge desk and Johnny found that he was looking at an urban survey map. In the top left hand corner was the title:

MULHOUSE: MAGINOT LINE.

Brizard started without further preamble:

"I have a package I want you to deliver and another to collect. Our package contains money and it will be sealed in that cigar box." As he spoke, he indicated an open, empty Dutch cigar box on the edge of the desk, square and deep. It would take a hell of a lot of money, thought Johnny. Brizard went on:

"You will go from Marseilles by light aircraft from the airport to a private field here, just outside Mulhouse. You will be met there by a man driving a grey van called Rouget, who will drive you to the rendezvous . . . here."

There was a pause while Brizard tried to trace the way to the spot, obviously unsure of the location. Calmet supplied the deficiency, stabbing his finger on it, and it seemed to Johnny that Brizard was irritated by his lieutenant's prompting:

"It is about two kilometres south of the main road, one of the old Maginot Line bunkers. You will be met there by two men. They will have the return package for you. You are not to hand over the money until you have made the pickup—understand?"

"Yes."

Brizard nodded with smiling approval:

"Good. Rouget will then drive you on to Lyon. There, as you should arrive shortly after dawn, you will catch the morning express and return that way to Marseilles. You should be back the same evening."

"When is all this going to happen."

"I want you to leave as soon as possible."

Johnny nodded:

"I'll just go and get my jacket."

"Study the map first."

It wasn't necessary, but Johnny made as if he was poring over the map for a few minutes. A man who has spent over a year in the bush of Central Africa with only the sketchiest of maps at his disposal, needs only a few seconds on a map crammed with urban landmarks, but it was better to make it look good.

While he was thus engaged, Brizard had opened his safe and he and Calmet were counting out wads of Swiss francs and packing them into the cigar box—as Johnny had speculated a few moments earlier, it was a hell of a lot of money.

As they finished counting the money and packing it, Brizard locked the safe, while Calmet shut the filled box, produced some sealing tape, sealed it, then slipped it inside an Air France bag that was lying on one of the chairs.

Johnny crossed the room:

"Okay, I won't be a second."

He was on the stairs before Calmet glanced at Brizard, got a curt nod from the other man, took the cigar box out of the bag and began to cut the seal as Brizard re-opened the safe.

Johnny was puzzled as he selected a leather jacket with a zip front—just the thing to keep him warm for an overnight job in northern France like this one. Yesterday, Brizard had paid him fifty thousand dollars for a simple killing, the same amount that Steve had handed over for the elimination of Brizard himself. Now, only the next day, he was ordering Johnny out on a courier job, the sort of routine handover that any of his thugs could have handled. He was on his guard, there must be more to it than met the eye.

He left his room, went along the corridor and started down the stairs. A moment of thought, then he turned, went back and knocked softly on Lucienne's door. After a moment, she opened it, a vision in a sheer black nightdress that covered her from neck to toe, but with a transparency that made it irrelevant. She leant forward, glanced up and down the corridor to see if it was empty, then kissed Johnny lightly:

"Good morning, kind sir."

Johnny responded, then:

"Listen, I have to do something for your father. I have to go away and won't be back until tomorrow night."

Lucienne frowned:

"Where are you going?"

"Just out of town. I'll call you when I get back." He kissed her again and walked down to the stairs. Lucienne stood in the doorway looking towards his retreating back, a frown of fear on her brow. As he reached the top of the stairs, Madame Apcar's door opened and she fluttered her false eyelashes at him.

He wondered whether she wore them in bed, as she was still dressed in a white version of Lucienne's night attire:

"Good morning."

"Good morning," returned Johnny.

She glanced up the corridor and saw Lucienne, who now had to pretend that she was leaving her room. As Johnny continued down the stairs he heard Madame Apcar say:

"Good morning, Lucienne darling. I have finally finished the guest list for the gala."

"Great," laughed Lucienne. "Did you remember to put me on it?"

"Of course." The sound of a door closing as Lucienne entered the bathroom.

The lower hallway was deserted and Johnny moved quickly and silently past the study door and into the front cloakroom. Once inside, he moved to the far end. The door that separated it from the study was fortunately ajar and he put his ear to it. He could hear Calmet moving around the room, but Brizard himself was on a phone call, giving orders rather than listening:

"Saturday night is my charity ball. I must be there at the beginning, but once I have made the rounds, I can slip away without anyone noticing, be with you at eleven o'clock and stay at least an hour until midnight."

He paused only for a second, then:

"Yes, an hour. That should give us time enough to complete the financial arrangements. I suggest you meet me outside the Buenos Aires at eleven o'clock precisely."

Again the pause, then his voice snapped:

"No—not in the Buenos Aires—outside . . . Very well, I'll see you on Saturday."

There came the sound of the receiver being replaced and Johnny turned quickly and went back out into the hall. He knocked on the door of the study and entered as Brizard called out. His eyes did not fail to notice that Calmet was once more slipping the cigar box into the travel bag. Brizard said:

"Are you ready?"

"Uh-huh."

"Good. You will leave your car here. Calmet will drive you to the airport. You can come straight here and report to me when you get back."

As he spoke, Calmet zipped up the bag and handed it to Johnny. The two men walked in silence down the villa steps and climbed into Calmet's car.

Johnny waited until they were on the coast road, making for the airport, before he spoke:

"What am I collecting."

Calmet snapped:

"Why do you want to know?"

Johnny shrugged:

"No reason, really. I just want to know what I should do if the police take an interest."

Calmet took his attention off his driving long enough to turn his head and fix Johnny with a piercing glare through the thick spectacle lenses:

"Now what makes you think the police would want to know about your trip?"

There didn't seem any answer to that, so Johnny relapsed into silence. Ten minutes later, they were at the airport and another half an hour after that, Johnny was in the air, the only passenger in a light private aircraft, flying north to Mulhouse.

At almost the moment of his take-off, the express from Paris was pulling into Marseilles main railway station and Steve Ventura, carrying only one small case, jumped off almost before it stopped.

It was early afternoon before Steve Ventura had his appointment with Chief Inspector Marsac and Inspector Farjas, the two officers who had been recommended to him by Inspector Briac before he left Paris.

Briac had wired ahead and they had acted with commendable efficiency. There had been a police car at the railway station, which drove him straight to the morgue to view the remains that had been identified as those of Johnny Deray. He had looked at them for a long time, trying to puzzle out where he had seen the shape of head before. The face was horribly disfigured, obviously mashed to a pulp by the fall but, equally obviously to Steve, this was not the body of Johnny Deray. The corpse was too lean, the skin too dark—and the hair was several shades darker than Johnny's muted blond.

He made no comment to the police about these discrepancies, it was a situation that he instinctively felt was best left secret for the moment. If Johnny had decided to swap identification with the dead man and go underground, then he obviously had good reason. Steve only hoped he could get to Johnny before he carried out the contract and killed Brizard.

The police sergeant who had met him at the station then took him to lunch after he had signed a statement formally agreeing that this was the body of Johnny Deray alias John Davos. The meal was a formal, almost silent affair, for Steve was determined not to pass on anything he knew about Brizard's nefarious plans until he was with Marsac and Farjas.

The appointment had been set for three o'clock and, punctually, Steve was conducted into Marsac's office. The office was empty, but a door on the far side opened as soon as the Sergeant had left the room by the way he had come and a man bustled in, closely followed by two other detectives. The first man identified himself at once, holding out his hand and introducing himself:

"Mr. Ventura, I am Inspector Marsac. I am so sorry to have kept you waiting."

"That's quite alright."

Marsac sat down at his desk and Steve glanced round at the other two men, who had remained standing by the door during his exchange with the Inspector. Marsac clapped his hands in a gesture of apology:

"I am sorry. This is Inspector Farjas and Inspector Pellegrin."

Farjas was a tall, stringy man, with a look of perpetual worry. Pellegrin was short and stocky, but with the same wary look of a working policeman round the eyes. Marsac said:

"Please sit down."

Steve shook his head and managed a wintry smile:

"I'd rather stand. I've been sitting rather a lot during the past twenty-four hours."

"As you prefer. Oh, could I see your identification?"

This was routine to Steve with police officers and departments who did not know him. He handed over his passport and Embassy credentials without demur. Marsac inspected them briefly, looking at the photograph and description in the passport and comparing them at a glance with the man in front of him, then he closed the passport and handed it and the identity documents back:

"Thank you. One can't be too careful, can one?"

Steve nodded:

"Not if you're a policeman."

Marsac smiled at the sally and turned to the other two men:

"Mr. Ventura of the American Embassy in Paris is asking for our co-operation. He comes highly recommended by Inspector Briac of the Paris Surete. Now, Mr. Ventura, exactly how can we help you?"

Steve leant forward on Marsac's desk:

"Mr. Marsac, I have information that a large shipment of drugs is on its way to Marseilles."

"What kind of drugs?" Marsac had exchanged a glance with his two colleagues and had now come fully onto the alert.

"Base morphine."

"How large?" It was Inspector Pellegrin who spoke, his voice harsh and deep.

As he replied, Steve did not for one second take his eyes off Marsac's face:

"Four hundred kilos."

Three men whistled through their teeth with surprise at the size of the shipment and Steve glanced round at them, more relaxed, knowing that he now had them hooked, Marsac glanced at Farjas and they exchanged almost imperceptible nods:

"Do you know who's buying it?"

Steve coloured and banged his fist down on the desk, angrily:

"We both know who's buying it."

"Who, Mr. Ventura?" Marsac's voice was very quiet, a note of warning in it, but Steve was too angry to notice it.

"Who buys all the junk that comes in through Marseilles? Jacques Brizard is who. Jacques Brizard is buying it."

There was a tense silence that was now broken by Farjas who stepped forward alongside the desk and asked, almost casually, as he leant against it:

"Do you have any other information for us?"

Steve was frankly taken aback that what he said so far should be taken so lightly—apart from the size of the actual shipment:

"Yes, I was coming to that. It's going to be delivered on the eighteenth of the month."

The three detectives exchanged renewed glances which seemed to say that the information was of little use to them. It was Marsac who spoke for the others, suddenly weary as if the interview had been a waste of time:

"Mr. Ventura, three of us have taken the trouble to see you because we understood you had important information for us. Is there anything you haven't told us?"

Steve was too surprised now to be angry:

"Four hundred kilos of base morphine isn't important?"

Marsac shrugged:

"We already knew about this shipment—all but the size of it, that is."

"You already knew," echoed Steve.

Marsac nodded:

"Please do not think you are the only person in France with reliable informers, Mr. Ventura. Inspector Farjas had all this information from an informer in the Port yesterday."

Steve asked anxiously:

"What else did he tell you?"

Farjas came forward, his face mirroring regret:

"Nothing. He was gunned down on the street shortly after I left him."

Steve nodded and sat down, suddenly one with the men around him. They seemed efficient honest policemen up against the same brick wall that he always hit in the end when he was pitted against Jacques Brizard:

"So, what's your next move?"

"Don't worry," shrugged Marsac. "We have Brizard under twenty-four hour surveillance."

"Under surveillance?"

"All we can do is wait."

Steve frowned:

"Have you tried tapping his telephone?"

Farjas smiled:

"We did try that once. It was discovered and neutralised within one hour. Now he moves around, makes calls from different places, has had landlines put in for his principal people, scrambler devices on them. It was not thought to be worthwhile—also there are other problems with it."

"Other problems?"

"Yes, you tap someone's line, a lot of people know of it. The magistrates have to counter-sign the orders. That way there is more chance of a leak, chance he will be informed of the moves we are making against him and will take simple precautions, like the cancellation of the shipment, or a change of date and venue for delivery."

Steve nodded briskly, heartened by the frankness of the other men. At least he was prepared to admit that there was an element of corruption to back up the charmed life of crime that Brizard led:

"Is there anything else you can do?"

Farjas and Inspector Marsac exchanged glances before both men shrugged. After a silence, it was Farjas who spoke:

"We can only do what we always do under the circumstances. Watch and wait for developments."

"Let's hope they include catching Brizard in possession during the delivery of the drugs." He turned as if to leave the office, but Marsac's voice pulled him up short, suddenly cold and brusque:

"Mr. Ventura. A moment."

He turned back, alert:

"Yes?"

"Could you explain to us your precise connection with the late Johnny Deray?"

Steve's answer was quick, perhaps too quick:

"He was an old friend."

"Are you aware that he has long been suspected—I should say was suspected and stress that it was only suspicion because there was never any proof against him—of being a top professional assassin."

Steve assumed what he hoped was a suitably blank expression:

"Johnny an assassin? God! That's ridiculous."

Marsac looked irritated:

"Nevertheless he died violently—and how were you so quickly informed, and why have you come here to check on his death."

Steve smiled, as if comprehension was dawning:

"Oh, I see. I was told by Inspector Briac. We were working together in Paris on this other matter, and, as he knew I was an old friend of Johnny's, he told me when the news came through."

"So you dropped your work on this drug thing to rush straight down here—knowing that your friend was dead?"

Steve shrugged:

"I was planning to come down about this drug thing anyway. I merely advanced my arrival a day or two. Somebody had to identify Johnny and make the arrangements for the funeral."

There was a tense silence in the office. Marsac glanced first at Pellegrin, then back to Farjas. He lowered his eyes and stared at his desk top, as if waiting for inspiration. He ended by nodding, more to himself than to the others:

"Alright. Thank you, Mr. Ventura. That is a reasonable explanation. I was sorry to show such suspicion, but as you yourself have implied it is always best to question and probe."

Steve nodded:

"Can I go now?"

Farjas spoke for his superior:

"Of course. We will keep you informed of any developments in the matter of the drugs."

"I see. Well, while we all watch and wait, do you mind if I take a look of my own around the City."

"Of course not," beamed Marsac. "But we have an old City. I hope you do not get lost."

"I have a map," snapped Steve, just before he closed the door on his questioners. He turned and started briskly down the corridor. At the lifts, he pressed and waited. It was then that Inspector Farjas appeared, waving a signal for him to wait. When he caught up with the American, he paused to take breath before saying:

"Please, I would like to give you a lift back to the hotel."

"No thanks, I can take a cab."

Farjas smiled, the look transforming his otherwise pale, worried features:

"Please. It will be so easy to go in my car. Anyway, there are things I would like to say to you and it will save time."

He winked as he spoke and Steve took the signal. They travelled down together in the lift and out into the police car park. Farjas led him to his personal vehicle, a battered Volkswagen. Steve smiled inwardly at the implication that the police are as badly paid in one country as in another.

It was only when they were in the car and underway that Farjas relaxed enough to mention what was on his mind:

"Mr. Ventura, I would like to be perfectly frank.

There are leaks in the Marseilles police department and it is difficult to talk with real freedom in front of one's colleagues, just in case, you understand. I have no reason to believe that my colleagues are amongst those at fault."

Steve smiled thinly:

"But how can I trust you—you might be the source of the leaks?"

Farjas nodded his head violently:

"That is rather what I mean. Still, it was my duty as a policeman to suspect myself. I investigated thoroughly and at least I am sure that we have nothing to fear from me."

Steve threw his head back and laughed out loud. He warmed at once to the man driving him. Farjas went on:

"Like you, I am not just in favour of sitting and waiting for events that may or may not occur on the eighteenth of the month. If we do that, one thing I am sure of, that Jacques Brizard will get his delivery and will get away with it with no trouble at all."

"What are you going to do?"

Farjas shrugged:

"I will watch and wait of course, like the others. But my watching and waiting will be a little less objective, will include something more positive. I would like to feel that I can keep you informed of any progress I make without compromising myself?"

Steve nodded, his mind racing. Taking his trust of the man in his hands, he said:

"Who is the body in the morgue?"

It was Farjas' turn to laugh:

"I thought as much. Like you, I knew it was not Johnny Deray in the morgue. It took a little while, but I believe it to be the body of an Algerian, a man called

Minieri. He disappeared a few days ago, then was reported returning from Paris—after that, nothing."

Steve's jaw fell slackly open:

"Minieri. But I met him in Paris. It was he who gave me the information about the eighteenth. I knew his shape was familiar."

"Uh-hu. I believe he came to you on Brizard's orders. It was a trap he was baiting for you perhaps. Even so he is dead and Johnny Deray's papers were found on him. Is Mr. Deray really your friend?"

Steve looked grim:

"Yes, whatever game he's playing, he's still my friend. I want no harm to come to him."

Farjas nodded violently again:

"Once, he was my friend too. Some years ago—the details do not matter—but I was in the force in Bordeaux at the time. The fact remains I would be loath to see him harmed also."

A moment later the battered Volkswagen turned in to the front ramp of the hotel and stopped. Steve reached over and shook Farjas by the hand, then stepped out. He walked round the car to enter the hotel, then Farjas stuck his head out of the driver's window:

"I am but a poor policeman. Still, it is my suspicion that Johnny Deray has been in Marseilles on business concerned with Jacques Brizard. Would that not be a solution?"

"A solution?"

"To the eighteenth. We both know what Johnny Deray does for a living."

"No," said Steve. "The legal way will be best if we can pull it off. I want Johnny stopped—but I don't want him harmed."

"But he is a clever man, Monsieur. Still if he can be stopped, it will be done. I will check with you in the morning in case there are any developments on these matters."

Steve stood on the steps, watching the policeman drive away. Then he turned to go through the massive doors of the hotel to register. He had chosen to stay at the Hotel Massena, the largest and most impressive hostelry in Marseilles, where, at that very moment, below stairs, frantic preparations were already underway for the biggest charity ball the City had ever seen—to take place on the night of the eighteenth, under the supervision of one of the City's leading citizens, Jacques Brizard.

It was dusk when Steve Ventura was finally able to lie down in his room to rest up after a hard day of travelling and questioning. As he stared up at the ornate ceiling of his room, he pondered on Johnny Deray and his present whereabouts. He also speculated how much trouble the killer might be in and hoped that none of the danger was due to his order to Briac to stop the contract. As he switched on the bedside light to alleviate the gloom, a whole country away a light aircraft circled once over a private field outside Mulhouse and the object of Steve's solicitude braced himself for the landing.

CHAPTER ELEVEN

Johnny glanced down at the deserted air strip below as the plane circled to make a final approach. The field consisted of two parallel runways and, some distance away, a small cluster of wooden huts, on one of which was a tall pole from which a limp wind-sock hung in the almost-still air. The field seemed deserted apart from a small van parked between the huts and the runways, beside which a man was leaning.

He felt a sense of relief as the plane touched down, a single squeal of tires on the under-carriage and a slight bump denoting the contact with terra firma. His nerves had been taut as a bowstring for the whole flight; the pilot, apart from glancing at him occasionally, had not uttered a word but had flown with a single-minded grim concentration which made Johnny, who had never liked flying much anyway, sink lower into his seat and pray that if there was a providence it was bent on keeping him in the air until they arrived at their destination.

The other reason for his tension was still clutched between his nerveless fingers—the flight bag containing the cigar box. Calmet had delivered him direct to the plane and the pilot would now deliver him direct to the driver who was to take him on to his destination, and so he would have no time alone to check the contents of the cigar box. After seeing Calmet put it away a second time just before they left Jacques Brizard's house, he was already suspicious and when the plane was airborne he had unzipped the bag, ostensibly to check the contents of overnight clothes and shaving kit. He had noticed then that the seal around the box had been broken and resealed, but he knew that if he inspected the contents the fact would be reported back to Calmet and Brizard by the pilot, thus blowing his cover with them.

All he was left with was an uncomfortable Hobson's choice, for whatever the box contained, he was convinced that it was not the money he had originally seen placed in it and he could only be on his guard and hope that he had not been led into a trap.

As the plane turned and came to a halt the man waiting by the truck threw away his cigarette and began to walk forward. Johnny turned to the pilot, who nodded to indicate that he could get down. He opened the cockpit passenger door and slid down to the ground, savouring the feeling of firm earth under his feet for a moment before ducking under the wing and walking towards the waiting man, the bag held tightly in his hand.

There came a roar from behind him as the plane started up again and began to taxi towards the airfield buildings and he ducked involuntarily as the wind of its propeller struck him.

As the man came level with him, Johnny asked:

"Rouget."

The man nodded and turned to walk alongside Johnny to the van. He was a thick-set, middle-aged man, dark and unshaven, with the typical looks and walk of a peasant. He did not speak, but his eyes kept glancing first at Johnny's face, then at the airline hold-all in his hand. It seemed to Johnny that everyone knew its significance except him.

As they reached the grey van, the plane turned and made its take-off down the runway. It soared into the air and Johnny watched it go before climbing into the passenger seat. He was on his own now, his only means of progress this not-to-be-trusted stranger and his old van.

Rouget climbed in, started the motor and the van jerked into action. Johnny hoped they would not have far to go. He could not stand the rattling he was getting and he had a feeling that the van wouldn't be able to operate under this stress for very much longer.

They drove round the buildings, then along a track which led to a tarmac road. The ride was better once they were on the road, but not much better. Johnny surveyed the darkening sky and glanced at his watch. It would certainly be dark long before they got to the rendezvous so he would have to check out his escape routes, in case they were needed, as best he could. This was one time when the principle of taking absolute care was essential; and one time when it could not be properly put into effect.

It was another hour before they reached their destination and, by that time, all the light had drained from the sky. Rouget, who had still not spoken, turned suddenly off the road, through a gap in the fencing and across a field. On the far side, there was another gap in the fence and Johnny speculated that this was a regular route they were taking across the grass. The van went slowly down a slope and, now out of sight of any traffic that might pass on the road, Rouget flashed on his headlights.

At the bottom of the slope stood an old concrete pillbox, the entrance to one of the old Maginot Line fortification bunkers. A short distance away was an old stone barn. The driver parked the truck close to the wall of the bunker, between the two buildings, switched off his engine and lights and sat quite still, not glancing at Johnny, not speaking.

After a few moments to get his eyes as accustomed as possible to the dark, Johnny opened his door and climbed down. The man turned to him and glanced at the hold-all. Johnny left it on the seat and set out to explore the contact area.

Besides the bunker entrance and the barn, there were no other buildings, but, on the far side of the barn a tarmac track came, presumably from another road to the north of them. It was from here that Johnny guessed their contacts would come. He returned to the van to see the driver climbing down. The man spoke for the first time:

"We are expected to flash the signal from the barn. Come."

Johnny went to the van and slipped the cigar box out of the travel bag, carrying it with him into the building. A large open window was set in the far wall and from it, Rouget was able to survey the track that approached it. He carried a torch in one hand, and kept glancing nervously at his watch. He said:

"They are due any time now."

Almost as he spoke there came a flash of headlights being turned rapidly on and off from some distance away. Rouget lifted the torch, flashed a reply and sighed with satisfaction as the signal was again returned. This time the car kept its lights on and began to move closer. When it was close enough for Johnny to make out that it was a black Citroen, he and Rouget turned and went to await its arrival in the space between the barn and the bunker, their backs to the van in which they had come. As the black Citroen came to a halt, Rouget breathed:

"Right on time."

There were three men in the car. The driver remained seated as the other two men climbed out and began to walk towards Johnny and his companion. Both wore trilby hats and mackintoshes against the cool of the night. There was something familiar to Johnny about their clothes and the way they walked, but he was off-balance and could not quite place it.

They halted a few yards away, then one of them took a pace forward and held out his hand:

"Have you got something for us?"

Johnny answered levelly:

"Do you have something for me?"

The man nodded and glanced back at his companion who produced a thick manila envelope from his inside pocket and handed it to his companion who walked forward, crossing the intervening gap. He and Johnny handed over their respective packages in unison. Johnny's nerves were honed to a fine edge, but even he was ill-prepared for what happened next.

As the packages exchanged hands, the man who had waited a little distance behind drew a revolver and called:

"You're under arrest."

A split second later, the headlights of the Citroen blazed on, half-blinding Johnny. In that second, he snapped:

"What for?"

He remained perfectly still as the man broke the tape and opened the cigar box, revealing two small packages of white powder—which Johnny recognised at once as heroin:

"Illegal possession of dangerous drugs."

Johnny took a pace forward and craned his neck as if to check the contents of the cigar box. The movement was so natural that it disguised his real intention for the seconds necessary for him to have placed the man holding it between him and the gun. Rouget had remained stock still throughout this, either a party to the betrayal, or too frightened to move. Johnny was not sorry; the man's inertia gave him all the more chance at surprise.

Johnny hurled the manila envelope in the man's face, then turned and ran to the cover of the van. In that instant, Rouget was moved into action, throwing the torch he still held at the man with the gun and diving for the cover of the barn. Behind the van, Johnny drew his gun as the first bullet ricocheted harmlessly off the side of the old, heavy metal vehicle.

He ducked back to fire in return and saw the two men making for cover at the side of the barn. Johnny fired two shots to help them on their way, then ducked down. If he was to have any chance of a getaway he would have to take out the headlights of the parked car, still bathing the scene in light as bright as daylight.

There was another volley of shots from the men in cover and Johnny ducked back, having located the car in his mind's eye. When he raised himself to fire, he was spot on. The bullet shattered the windscreen and killed the driver of the car instantly. He ducked back, his new aiming spot in his mind and waited for the inevitable return shots to pass overhead before jumping once more and pumping the rest of his magazine into the petrol tank of the Citroen.

There was an explosion and a whoomp of noise as the car burst into flames. He saw the two men stand and turn involuntarily to watch the fire and took the opportunity to open the door on the covered side of the van. He crawled in on the floor, found the leads under the dashboard, pulled them out. More bullets came, one glancing off the bonnet, painfully close to the windscreen. A moment of feverish groping and Johnny had short-circuited the starting mechanism and the van roared into life. Johnny heaved himself up on the driver's seat, dropping his now empty gun on the floor. As he raised his head, there came a fusilade of shots, one of them cracking, but not shattering the windscreen. Johnny jammed the van into reverse and pressed his foot down hard on the accelerator. The van shot backwards and began to go up the slope. Johnny slammed it into forward gear and did a roaring turn on the slope. For a moment the van teetered as if about to keel over, then righted itself. Johnny charged off up the slope into the darkness, leaving the area of the shooting bathed in the orange glow of the still burning car.

It was only as he shot out on the road and turned the van south that he remembered Rouget and felt a moment of regret. After all, the man had thrown his torch at the policeman holding the gun and had made a run for it. He could not have been in on the betrayal, but was an innocent victim of the treachery of Jacques Brizard himself.

A moment later he dismissed the incident from his mind and his brain raced over the possibilities of escape. He would probably be safe for an hour at least. When he had checked the map in the study he had seen that the rendezvous point was in a particularly deserted area, so the two policemen, without transport or radio communication, destroyed in the burning car, would take a while to inform their superiors of what had occurred—probably hampered by having to take Rouget in with them.

He debated in his mind whether he could get to

Lyon as originally planned before a full-scale alert had reached the proportions necessary for the police to be on the look-out for the van at that distance. He gunned the vehicle forward, switching on the lights. He calculated that he would have the hours of darkness to put as much distance between himself and Mulhouse as possible, but that, after dawn, he would be taking a grave risk.

He drove like a madman all through the night, joining the Mennecy road into Lyon at just about daybreak. For the first time, he was in traffic, the road consisting of four lanes separated by a central reservation on which trees were dotted at intervals. As the sun rose, Johnny groped in his pocket and slipped on his sunglasses.

It was about an hour after dawn that he was spotted by the police as he drove down the road. The van was in the outside lane, overtaking a lorry, other traffic behind. The manoeuvre successfully hid from him the small police car parked in a layby, but, as the van went past, the policemen started their engine, switched on the blue light and moved into the traffic, weaving between cars and lorries to catch up with him.

It was about two vehicles behind when Johnny spotted it. He knew at once that there was no way to beat the police car except by out-driving it, so he did not speed up, merely watched carefully in his mirror as it made the last lane changes that put it alongside him. After a moment, it shot past, then skidded in front of him, causing him to stop. He had been expecting the manoeuvre, so pulled up a good deal short of the police car, leaving him room to get round it if that should prove the best way.

The two policemen climbed out, slamming their doors, and moved towards the van, both unbuckling the cover guards on their gunbelts. Johnny let them come forward two or three paces, then gunned the van. Traffic passing in the inside lane made it impossible for him to go in that direction, so he swung the wheel, roared over the central reservation and continued to go south into the twin streams of the oncoming traffic.

He was past the police before they had time to recover themselves and run back to their vehicle. He knew he would have another thirty seconds while they opened and closed doors and got started and this might give him the time he needed, provided his reflexes remained good enough to dodge the oncoming traffic.

The best way to travel against the traffic flow was by the most frontal method. He took a line down the middle of the road, straddling the white line between lanes, and forcing the cars and lorries in each lane to swerve to avoid him, before closing up beyond him, blocking the occupants of the now chasing police car from getting a good shot at his tires.

Then he heard the siren and realised that his ruse had not been entirely successful. The two policemen who had been so easily tricked were now speeding along the other side of the road, keeping parallel with him, their light flashing, the siren blaring.

Johnny looked ahead. A short distance away he would come to the intersection where he was due to turn off to the right towards Lyon. Still determined to stick to his original plan, he prepared himself for the swing to the right, across the intersection and the traffic travelling in the same direction as himself. The police car was still neck and neck.

He dodged round a lorry on the far side, then screamed back across both oncoming lanes as the intersection was reached. He abruptly turned the wheel to the right to take the corner.

At the same moment his pursuers reached the intersection and turned left to come across into oncoming traffic and block him off. He was a split second ahead of them in his timing. The police car hit him a glancing blow in the rear. As Johnny desperately struggled with the wheel to keep the van on course, the other car spun round, skidded across the road into the oncoming traffic, to be hit sideways on by a lorry. It turned over and came to rest against an embankment wall on the far side of the road, still upside down, its occupants trapped inside. Johnny slowed down long enough to drink in the scene in the rear-view mirror before putting his foot on the accelerator and speeding up towards Lyon. With any luck they would not even have had time to alert headquarters over the radio that they had spotted him and had given chase.

The side road was empty as he sped towards the railway station and the train to Marseilles. He glanced at his watch. He would be in plenty of time for it, and there was no point in getting caught in a motorcycle speed trap. After all, it was the one unlucky time you didn't out-think the opposition that you would get caught and, unlike most men who work in the shadows beyond the law, Johnny, though he might not trust policemen, still had a healthy respect for them.

He arrived in Lyon with a good fifteen minutes to spare and drove the van into the station car park, slotting it into a space by the wall, the furthest point from the road. He strolled nonchalantly on to the platform, purchased his ticket and strolled down the almost-deserted tarmac until he saw the sign for the gentleman's rest room. He spent the time waiting for the train locked in one of the booths. There was no point in tempting providence with more exposure than he had to.

The train was on time and Johnny found himself an

empty carriage and settled down for the Express journey back to Marseilles and Jacques Brizard. The journey would give him time to think through the events of the past three days, and also plan his next moves.

It was obvious that Brizard was out to get him—the only question would be why? Was it because his cover was broken and the gang boss knew his real identity and the purpose of his visit to Marseilles? On balance, Johnny thought not. They would have acted directly and more decisively on him if that had been the case. Certainly Brizard would not have risked his daughter being alone with him, away from the protection of the villa.

Lucienne, now that was stronger ground. Johnny had sensed the bond of affinity between them from the first moment he had seen them together. Lucienne was a normal, healthy girl—very normal, very healthy—who was loving and dutiful to her father. But his attitude to her was the key. To say that he doted on her would not be an exaggeration. Johnny's elimination could be quite on the cards, if Brizard thought that he was stealing his daughter's affection.

He grinned to himself as he watched the countryside flash by, sombre under lowering skies. He had certainly gone straight for Brizard's achilles heel. The only problem was that it had placed him in greater danger than his quarry. Still, she remained a useful card to play.

Johnny frowned as he turned his mind to his other problem—Steve Ventura and Inspector Briac. He had always trusted Steve, ever since their ordeal together in the Congo, and he knew that the other man would not jeopardise him except accidentally, acting from the best of motives. Johnny determined to call the number the American had given him as soon as he was safely in Marseilles.

This last thought took his mind onto more immediate problems. By now, there was no way in which Brizard could still be uninformed of the failure of his betrayal. Johnny would be surprised if the railway station in the City was not crawling with his men. For my next trick, thought Johnny, I will spirit myself through them—somehow. He could think of no good way while he was on the train, he would just have to make the circumstances work for him when he arrived in the City.

Johnny was standing in the corridor as the train pulled in to Marseilles station. By squinting along the platform through the glass, he spotted Henri and Kurt straight away. They were standing at the end of the platform, waiting to scrutinise each passenger as he or she went past. The train stopped and doors opened, disgorging the passengers who hurried towards the end of the platform intent on leaving the station. Johnny had picked a position about half-way up the train, just ahead of the guard's van and, as he watched and waited, the van was opened and a porter appeared driving a small electric truck, the usual trailers hooked on to the back.

At the van he was joined by two or three colleagues, who piled the trailers high with mailbags and parcels. The driver got aboard and started to take his load down the platform.

As the trailers went past the doors of Johnny's carriage, he stepped down and walked alongside the highest-piled one, before picking his moment and jumping into a clear space on it, pulling down one of the mailbags to give him cover on his blind side.

He smiled. It was one of the oldest tricks in the book, but it worked like a dream. He was whisked past Henri and Kurt without them giving it a second glance. Obviously, Brizard and Calmet kept them too busy to go to the pictures.

As the trailers reached the main concourse and one of the yawning exits that led into the blazing Mediterranean sunshine, Johnny jumped off and, holding the airline holdall in one hand so that he could use it as a flail if necessary, he darted to the entrance and began to run down the steps.

The car park outside Marseilles railway station is set high above the old town. From it, a road winds down to the town itself, but, for the convenience of pedestrians there is a flight of stone steps that also leads down to the roads below. Johnny spotted Calmet at once as his car came to a halt close to the steps and he jumped out of the passenger seat.

Johnny ran forward, ramming Calmet's door, forcing it into him, pinning him to the side of the car and causing him to cry out with shock and pain. He had expected his quarry to run, not to attack, and his surprise was compounded as the travel bag caught him on the side of the head, stunning him momentarily.

Johnny ran on to a clump of motor-cycles and mopeds parked in a little group near the steps. His keen eye spotted one that was not chained and he jumped on it, kick-started it and backed out of the cluster. Calmet was just recovering from the attack and made a grab for Johnny as he drove past, missing him by the narrowest margin. The cycle then mounted the pavement and, with a short prayer to St. Christopher, Johnny launched himself down the steps.

Helplessly Calmet watched him go. There was no way in which the car could follow and, by the time it got down the road, Johnny would have disappeared into the labyrinth of the old town and would be practically impossible to locate. He turned and walked angrily into the station to fetch Kurt and Henri and to find a phone from which to alert Brizard.

He was in no happier frame of mind when he had finished the call. Brizard had been furious at his failure, but had ordered him to put the string of informers that he ran onto locating Johnny. Somewhere in the City—most probably in the old Algerian quarter, Johnny would have to find a hotel room and go to earth. Calmet privately thought that it was a more likely bet that the fugitive would put as much space between himself and Marseilles as he could, but he did not voice this opinion out loud over the phone.

Instead, he remained in the booth from which he had made the call to Brizard, and started setting the search in motion; the whole process from the chief informers to the junkies and petty crooks, all of whom owed favours to Brizard and his men; spreading the word so that Johnny could go nowhere in the City without being spotted. It took a scant fifteen minutes.

When he left the booth Calmet was smiling his thin humourless smile. There was no way, if Johnny was still in Marseilles, that he could escape the net. Calmet could reasonably hope that by sunset the man would be dead.

CHAPTER TWELVE

When he escaped into the old town from the railway station, Johnny made for what he thought was the safest place in Marseilles—the beach. He spent the rest of the afternoon sitting on the plage, watching the children playing at the edge of the waves. It was at times like this, the times of maximum danger, that Johnny liked to watch children, the innocents of the world, the people to whom people like him were shadows in a cinema, or on a television screen or words in a book. As he watched them, he tried to blank everything out of his mind but the job in hand and the problems he now faced.

He was under no illusions. His escape from Calmet was but a brief respite. To a man as highly organised as Jacques Brizard, finding one man in Marseilles would not be difficult. He would have eyes on every street corner, in every shop and bar. His only chance was to find some small hotel and hole up for a few hours while he got rested and ready for the fray.

He bought a paper at a small news kiosk and read it

casually. It was only as he folded it to throw it in a nearby litter bin that he realised the date—it was the seventeenth, the following night would be the night of the Charity Gala and the night of the drug delivery that he had overheard in the hall washroom of Brizard's villa. He knew that between now and the time of the delivery, he would have to contact Steve Ventura and get his help. He had always boasted that he never needed anyone, but now, he thought grimly, he needed all the help he could get and Steve was the one person to give it to him. After all, what were friends for.

Now that he had an objective in mind, the next moves came easily to him. He went into a small junk shop on the quay and purchased a battered suitcase, filling it with newspaper that he had obtained from the litter bin. Then he started a tramp up the side streets, dark glasses covering his face in spite of the coming of dusk. Most of his money was hidden in the boot of his car with his guns, now stuck at Brizard's villa, but he had a good amount in his wallet and, when he reached a row of shops, he purchased new shirts, shoes and ties as well as an off-the-peg suit and overcoat. It was not of the quality that he normally wore, but they were smart and new enough to look good for as long as he thought was necessary—the next twenty-four hours.

The suitcase was convincingly heavy when he finally picked on a hotel that seemed most likely to suit his needs. A dilapidated sign above the door, half its neon letters broken, announced to a disinterested world that the establishment was called the Hotel Miami. Johnny pushed in through the narrow swing doors and found himself immediately in what would be described as the games room of the hotel. At least, there was a shabby billiard table, two men playing away patiently as he walked round them and to the tiny desk where an aged concierge sat knitting. She did not even look up as he stood in front of her. He cleared his throat:

"Do you have a room, please?"

The old woman stopped knitting for long enough to turn round the tattered registration book and point to a space where Johnny might register. He took a broken pen from a holder on the desk, both pen and holder covered in a layer of grime, and signed his name: Johann Schmidt. He was confident that this was one establishment that would not ask for him to leave his passport at the desk as a means of registration and identification. He was not wrong.

He turned the book back and this time the woman was good enough to give it a cursory glance. One talon-like hand reached out, grabbed a key off a hook and threw it down on the desk in front of him. He picked it up:

"Thank you—oh, do you have a phone."

For the first time the old woman was forced to abandon her knitting altogether to pay attention to her customer. As she looked at him, her watery blue eyes looking as if she could not even make out more than his shape, he was reminded of those old films about the French Revolution. The women knitting by the guillotine were probably her ancestors—she couldn't be quite old enough to have been there herself. She pointed with one of her emaciated hands to a phone that was hung on the wall, before leaning forward, wheezily opening a drawer in her desk and producing a jeton which she threw on the counter. Johnny put some change down for the token:

"Thank you."

She nodded acknowledgement, too surprised at his good manners to glare for a moment, and he turned and went to the phone. He placed the jeton and dialled his number. He smiled as Lucienne answered the phone. The first part of the gamble was paying off:

"Hello, hello?"

He said quietly:

"Lucienne?"

"Yes—Johnny—where are you?"

He paused for a moment, then realised he was over-anxious, over-reacting. She was merely worried that he had not returned as promised to the villa that morning:

"Never mind about that for a moment. I want you to meet me—can you get away?"

She was silent for a moment, then:

"I don't know. It's difficult. Father—he is nervous about something. Why don't you come to the villa."

"No. I don't want to come there."

"Why not?"

"I can't explain for the moment, but not there. Couldn't you come to the yacht club?"

"Why the yacht club?"

"Listen, I'll explain when I see you. Come to the parking lot at the yacht club in—say forty-five minutes, okay?"

He waited, holding his breath for her reply. She was suddenly very important to him, it was suddenly absolutely necessary that she come. It seemed that he had been hanging on for her reply for an eternity when she finally spoke:

"Alright."

He sighed:

"Okay, goodbye."

"Goodbye," she breathed back as he broke the connection.

He walked back to the desk and picked up the key the woman had dropped there. Then he picked up his suitcase and walked to the shabby staircase that led to the land of box-sized promise that was the Hotel Miami.

In his room, which he was relieved to see was not quite as dirty as the public quarters of the hotel, he changed into his new suit. He slipped his gun into his inside pocket and was ready to go. The next thing he would need was a car, then to get to the yacht club.

He locked his room carefully and went back downstairs, handing in his key at the desk with a mocking politeness that caused the woman to abandon her knitting once more and take it. He nodded and gave a polite 'thank you' before walking past the same two unshaven men who were still concentrating on the billiard table.

It was only when he got outside and into the street that he quickened his pace and began to look around for a suitable vehicle in the darkened streets. As he looked he walked in the general direction of the yacht club—there was no point in wasting any time.

Jacques Brizard was not wasting any time either. He had locked himself in his study while he made the final preparations and called his partner regarding the pick-up of the dope on the following night. On one corner of his desk he had a monitoring extension on which he could listen in to any call that came to the villa without the speakers being aware they were being overheard. A light appeared below the speaker, and Brizard turned the switch which tuned in the conversation. It was almost a reflex action and he continued with his own work until he heard Johnny's voice. He stiffened and listened to the whole conversation, recognising the concern in his daughter's voice as she asked Johnny where and how he was. He felt an uncontrollable anger welling up in him that this cheap crook should be getting a hold on his daughter.

As soon as the call was over he turned the dial and picked up the direct line to Calmet's apartment. He had allowed his lieutenant an early night in preparation for the next day. The phone was picked up almost at once:

"Mr. Brizard?"

Brizard waited for a moment until he was sure he had his anger under control. It never did to show stress:

"Calmet, I am sorry to disturb you, but I have a little job for you to arrange."

His voice was almost too slack and calm. Calmet was alerted at once. As calm as this, Brizard was always at his most dangerous:

"What do you want me to do."

"Deray is meeting my daughter at the yacht club in about forty minutes. Arrange to have a man there. Then come to the house. We will go to dinner at the yacht club later—understood?"

"Understood Monsieur Brizard." The connection was broken. Brizard sat back and allowed himself a moment of relaxation. Calmet really knew his job. He and the men he picked were thorough professionals.

The car that Johnny finally settled on was an almost new black Citroen. It was a lucky choice; he did not even have to wire the ignition, a spare set of keys were lying on the glove compartment and the driver's door was unlocked.

He drove to the yacht club and let the powerful car glide into the parking lot. He settled near the entrance and waited for Lucienne to arrive. After a few minutes he was glad to have been a little early.

A Renault 16 came along the street, past the entrance to the parking lot, and pulled up in a pool of light in front of the yacht club. In the light Johnny was able to see, even at that distance, that the driver was Henri. He waited for Henri to get out of the car and go into the deserted entrance to the club, but nothing happened, the man just sat and waited.

A few moments later, there was a roar from a powerful engine, a flash of light that streaked round the corner and Lucienne's Porsche came into the car park. She drove once round the park until she had located Johnny sitting in the Citroen, then parked next to it, jumped out and ran over to Johnny's car. She opened the passenger door, jumped in and slammed it behind her.

For a few moments the world receded—Henrí parked in his car down the street, Brizard's men on the look-out for him all over Marseilles—even Brizard himself and all he could feel was her hot breath, her lips on his, her body pressed against him. They kissed, then she broke away:

"Why didn't you come back to the villa. Father was worried about you when you didn't turn up."

"I'll bet he was."

"That's not fair, Johnny. He likes you, he told me so after that first day—why else did he have you work for him?"

Johnny smiled at her in her innocence:

"Okay, tell him I'm fine and not to worry about me"

"Why don't you tell him yourself?"

Johnny frowned. He didn't want to tell Lucienne what had happened. Probably she wouldn't believe that her father could be a criminal.

"I will when I see him."

Lucienne reached across and nibbled his ear:

"Come back now and see him, with me. I know he'd like you to—and you know what I think."

For a moment he responded, kissing her hard. Over

the top her head as they broke he could see that Henri was still sitting inert in his car outside the yacht club. A sudden thought crossed his mind. It would help him considerably if he was to know where Brizard would be for the rest of the night. He didn't like using Lucienne as an unwitting tool in his fight with her father, but one must use what tools are to hand in such a situation:

"Say, you wouldn't happen to know where your Father is right now, would you?"

Lucienne said:

"Oh, he's got a meeting at the house, he and Monsieur Calmet—then he's coming here right after."

"Here?"

"Yes, to the yacht club."

"What for?"

Lucienne laughed and frowned at the same time:

"You are funny, Johnny. He's coming here to eat, of course." He felt relief flood through him. Her answer was spontaneous enough. She didn't know that her Father planned to eliminate him. He asked one more question:

"What time."

"Look, this is silly. He'll be here soon. He's coming here to dinner and then going back home after to see a football game on television. Let's go in to the club now. We can have a drink while we wait for him and then eat with him."

Johnny held her closer:

"No. I want to see him alone. We have some private business together."

"All right. I'll stay here with you until he arrives. Then you can meet with him and we'll all eat afterwards."

To Johnny, who wanted no direct confrontation with Jacques Brizard that night, her suggestion was the last thing he needed. Further, he now had it in his mind to take out Henri as a warning to the crime king and he didn't want Lucienne around to witness that. He ran his hands down her body to her waist, feeling her breath come faster as his touch aroused her, bringing her closer to him. His voice was slow, suggestive:

"No. Why don't you go back to the villa for the moment. It's going to get very cold out here."

Her hands went to his shirtfront as she unbuttoned the shirt, her fingetips running over his chest. Then she put her head down and began to kiss and lick at his skin, whispering:

"Have you ever made love on the front seat of a Citroen?"

He held her face in his hands, forcing her back off him so that he could look directly into her eyes:

"Yes, I have. But I have a much better idea."

She pressed as close as she could. He could feel her hands on his thigh. He didn't think her idea was too bad either. It was just that the job—and his life—came first. As a professional he was not proud of himself. He had bungled the Contract right the way down the line so far. Now he had a last chance to put things right and he wasn't going to louse it up:

"Why don't you go home, get into a nice hot bath, turn the lights down low . . . Cover yourself with lots of perfume and slip between smooth silk sheets."

She was breathing hard with excitement, trying to reach her face up to his as he cupped it firmly in his hands:

"And then?"

He kissed her lightly on the forehead:

"And I'll see you as soon as I've finished with your father," he ended with a bright smile.

He let go of her, leant across and opened the car door:

"Okay, on your way."

She held his arm:

"When will you come?" It was as if she knew that there was a chance that he would never be able to.

He kissed her again by way of reply, with all the passion he could muster. It seemed to satisfy her as an answer because she slipped out of the car and with a smile and a wave got into her own, started it and roared off into the night.

Johnny watched her go, until her lights had disappeared round the bend. Then the softness went from his face and he became the ice-cold professional again. Henri still sat in the car, unmoved and unmoving.

Johnny groped for a moment in his pocket. He had placed a small package of chalk in it and now he took this out and rubbed a little into the palm of his right hand. If he fired the gun, then washed the chalk away, there would be no sign of powder burns on his hand. He took out his gun, checked it and put it in the side pocket of his coat. In the darkness the bulge would not show and he would surely signal his intentions to his quarry if he had to reach into his inside pocket for the weapon.

He waited for a moment, deliberately clearing his mind and relaxing his body so that he would be ready to kill quickly and without compunction. The worst enemy a professional killer faced was tension while in the act of doing the job. Since he had met Lucienne, Johnny felt that he had let far too much tension seep into his thoughts and his decision-making. It had endangered his life, and at that moment he felt more vulnerable than ever he had done in the Congo bush.

Primed and ready, he climbed out of the Citroen and loudly slammed the door so that there would be no chance that Henri would not notice him in the gloom. He walked from the car park and, once on the pavement, he turned away from the yacht club and began to walk slowly down the street. Henri took his cue like a dream, Johnny heard the Renault start up, then the smooth hum of his engine as he kerb-crawled towards him.

As the victim who thought he was to be a killer came alongside, he wound down his window. Johnny turned as if only just aware that he had been followed and was greeted with an affable smile from the car driver:

"Excuse me."

"Yes."

Inside the car, Henri had a map on his lap. Johnny knew instinctively that he was holding a gun underneath it:

"Can you tell me how to get to the Avenue of the Republique. I seem to be lost." He had one hand in view and he stabbed it at the map. Johnny, acting as if he suspected nothing and was really dealing with a man who needed help and directions leant into the car. At the same time, out of sight, hidden by the line of the door, he slipped his own gun out of its pocket and held it against the door, so that it would fire upwards at Henri's head.

The gun in Henri's lap came up, moving the map and, in that moment, Johnny fired twice, in quick succession. Henri slumped back, dead, as Johnny slipped the gun back into his pocket and pointed at the map.

"Yes. It's just there."

He turned abruptly and walked briskly back to his stolen car. He knew very well that Henri would not be alone, that one of the others would be on the scene in a few moments. He jumped in the car and roared off down the road, suddenly amused to see Kurt dart out of a side street, struggling to get a pistol from his pocket.

It was half an hour before Jacques Brizard's Rolls-Royce glided round the corner and came to a halt in the open space at the yacht club entrance. Brizard was sitting in the back with Madame Apcar. Calmet sat in the front passenger seat and Wilson was at the wheel. A few yards ahead of them, down the road, an ambulance shed its eerie blue light over the scene. There were also two police cars and a small crowd, all grouped round a Renault 16.

As Brizard climbed out and stared at the small crowd, the ambulance doors were shut and the vehicle pulled away. At the same time, Kurt came out of the small crowd of onlookers and Calmet got out of the Rolls and went to speak to him. Brizard watched, eagle-eyed, as he helped Madame Apcar down from the car, almost depositing her in the road so fixed was his concentration on his lieutenant's meeting.

Kurt was frightened.

"We did everything as you instructed, but Deray . . ."

He stopped as Calmet turned abruptly on his heel and joined Brizard and Madame Apcar at the entrance to the club. Brizard pushed Madame Apcar ahead of him into the entry hall, then turned to Calmet, his face a mask:

"Find out what happened. Don't join me till you do."

He turned on his heel and went inside. Calmet walked back to Kurt, his face reflecting his master's fury:

"Alright. Tell me."

Kurt could feel the line of sweat on his brow, and hoped his fear did not show in the darkness:

"I was supposed to make my way to that alley opposite and hide in the shadows of the entrance while Henri drove down here and waited for Deray to come—."

Calmet's harsh voice cut across his hesitant words: "I know all that—I told you what to do. I just want to know what went wrong?"

Kurt shrugged:

"Deray was too fast, and—." Calmet's hand came up with lightning speed and caught Kurt across the face with a vicious backhand slap that made a noise like a pistol crack in the rapidly emptying street. He brought his hand back immediately and hit his hireling again, then a third time. Kurt braced himself. Now that the manifestation of displeasure had come, he was no longer afraid. It was always like this when he knew how he stood.

Calmet was breathing heavily after his violent movement. He waited a moment to recover himself, then:

"All that happened was that you were too slow—find him."

"But how?"

Calmet's face was twisted with rage, an unwonted show of emotion, naked and frightening:

"Must I tell you everything. Check the hotels and bars. All the informers. They have been on the lookout for him all afternoon. Someone must know something. I don't want to hear from you until Johnny Deray is dead—understood?"

"Understood."

He was trembling as he saw Calmet stride into the club. He needed a moment to recover his composure before moving off on an errand that he looked upon as foolhardy suicide. For, standing in the entrance ot the alley, he had watched Johnny Deray kill his companion. Kurt might have been a slow man, but he knew and recognised a true professional when he saw one.

Calmet walked straight past the desk at the yacht

club, into the restaurant and over to Brizard's table. A place had been laid for him facing his boss, Madame Apcar between them. Brizard looked up from his soup:

"Well?"

Calmet nodded:

"We are taking care of it. Johnny Deray is a dead man."

CHAPTER THIRTEEN

After his long journey from Paris to Marseilles and his almost day-long session with the police, Steve Ventura had spent the night when Johnny had escaped from the trap at Mulhouse in restless sleep. He was unused to the heat of the City and his mind was still teeming with the information and remarks of Inspector Farjas in the car as he had given him a lift to the hotel.

The next morning he still felt tired and this, combined with his frustration and impatience made him a bad-tempered man to run into. He did not care to leave the hotel in case Farjas called him with some information and so he spent the whole day in a torment of worry. It was the seventeenth—only one day to go before Brizard could be locked into a consignment of drugs and arrested—if there were no slip-ups.

As the day progressed, and there was no call, Steve's spirits sank all the more. He was none too sanguine of the chances of picking up Brizard and making a charge stick. If even a man like Farjas was afraid to speak too loudly for fear of information getting back to the gang leader, then Brizard must have the whole city in his pocket.

He was also worried that there was no news from Johnny, but this situation was righted late in the day when Marsac called him:

"Mr. Ventura. I am sorry to disturb you, but we've had a puzzling report."

"Yes?"

"The man Deray," he paused and Steve said cautiously:

"But he is dead."

It was Marsac's turn to pause on the line:

"Is there any chance that you were mistaken?"

Steve saw his chance to get off the hook if there was any backlash later. He guessed rightly that the conversation was being recorded:

"Well, there's a chance, of course. I mean, the face was so horribly mutilated."

"I see." The voice sounded disappointed, as if Marsac had hoped to pin him with a denial. "Well, we've had a report from Mulhouse and Lyon."

"But they're in northern France?"

"Yes. That is what is even more puzzling. A man answering Deray's description was the subject of an arrest attempt by special Sureté Agents at a Maginot Line bunker near Mulhouse."

"Was the attempt successful?" Steve tried to keep the anxiety out of his voice.

"No." Marsac was brusque. "One officer was killed when his car was blown up by a bullet in the petrol tank, one of the other two was wounded. The man answering Deray's description escaped. In the morning he was spotted by a police patrol on the road coming south. He escaped again and the patrolmen are in hospital, but they will live. The van the fugitive was travelling in was found an hour ago in Lyon station yard."

Steve breathed a silent sigh of relief, then:

"But why were you informed?"

"Because the information that led to the attempted arrest at Mulhouse came from an informer in the Marseilles area. Also the Marseilles Express stops at Lyon, and had passed through the city shortly before the van was spotted."

"What are you going to do—wait for the train at Marseilles station."

He heard Marsac's sigh:

"We were informed too late. The train had already arrived. There was some sort of scuffle outside the railway station and a motor bicycle was stolen. The man escaped. I have to tell you, Monsieur, that, if John Deray is still alive, he is in Marseilles."

"Thank you for letting me know," said Steve. Then the connection was broken.

Steve went into the hotel bar to have a celebration drink. All round him were the signs of the preparations for the huge charity ball that Brizard was to throw the following night, but now these failed to depress Steve as he toasted Johnny's nine lives.

His euphoria lasted only a few minutes. By the time he had eaten a solitary dinner and had got through the main part of the evening by reading magazines in the hotel lounge before retiring for another sleepless night, he was once more in a state of depression. There was no way he could get in touch with Johnny. There was, of course, a chance that the police would pick him up, but it would have to be almost by accident, as they had failed conspicuously so far. He fell at last into a fitful sleep, wishing for calls from both Johnny and the police inspector.

It was Farjas who was the first to grant his wish. He

called at five o'clock in the morning and seemed full of energy, as if he had already been up for hours:

"Can you be dressed and ready in half an hour?"

Steve wiped the sleep from his eyes and looked out at the greyness of the pre-dawn sky:

"Why? Where are we going?"

"My men are searching the docks. I thought you might like to come with me."

Steve cursed, but still swung himself out of bed:

"But that's routine, surely. You don't expect to find anything that way, do you?"

"Perhaps not," chuckled the policeman. "But I have some other news for you."

He put down the phone at once, making Steve anxious for the meeting so that he dressed and changed in double-quick time. He was in the lobby ten minutes later to see if he could get a cup of coffee before the policeman arrived, but to his surprise Farjas was waiting for him in the hall. He smiled as he walked Steve out to the car:

"I lied about the half hour. I took the liberty of ringing you up from the lobby."

In spite of the earliness of the hour and a pounding headache that had come in the wake of his restless sleep, Steve found himself smiling and warming further to the man. He really was beginning to like and trust him.

A police car was waiting on the steps and, as they climbed in, Farjas asked:

"Have you got anything since the day before yesterday?"

"Yeah, a headache."

Farjas laughed as the car moved off and started in the direction of the huge complex of docks:

"What do you prefer—an aspirin or some information?"

"How about both."

To his surprise, Farjas took some aspirin tablets from his pocket and handed them to the American. Steve swallowed two, then Farjas went on:

"That is the first. As to the second, well, you know about the incident at Mulhouse and the fugitive now being positively identified as Johnny Deray."

Steve nodded:

"That much I do know—and that Deray is now back in Marseilles—and that the police have so far been unable to pick him up—am I right?"

Farjas was silent for a moment, digesting the tone of anger that underlay Steve's apparently calm words:

"You are right as far as it goes. But we have more on Mr. Deray now."

"What?"

"Last night there was an incident near the yacht club—the club owned by Mr. Brizard. A man was found shot in the driving seat of a small Renault car. His name was Henri and he worked for Mr. Brizard."

"I've run across him," said Ventura grimly, remembering the chase in the Paris Metro when Brizard's men had been out to kill him.

"Well, even the French police can be efficient when they have a mind. The bullet that killed him was from the same gun that wounded the policeman at Mulhouse. John Deray did the murder."

Steve was more cautious, on behalf of his friend:

"If indeed it was he who was at Mulhouse."

"It is as you say, Monsieur. Legally we have no proof, it still has to be sorted out. Perhaps we never will have. Nevertheless, I told you because it makes it all the more certain that Johnny Deray is back in Marseilles."

They had reached the dock area and Farjas asked Steve to remain in the car for a while. He got out and went to confer with a group of senior uniformed officers who were obviously waiting for him by the dock gates. Steve glanced at his watch. It was nearly half past six. Another hour and the docks and the City would have sprung magically to life. Now there were only the scurrying forms of the police going from ship to ship, inspecting the cargoes on the quayside and entering and leaving the warehouses and bonded stores.

Farjas came back to the passenger side of the car and opened the door as an invitation to Steve to climb out and join him. As the big American heaved himself from the car, he asked if anything had been found. Farjas shrugged:

"Nothing yet. But I have told them to continue the search. There is not much hope really. Anyway, we would rather find it tonight when Brizard can be tied in to it, though I have some bad news about that as we seem to be alone in our conviction."

Steve glanced, sharp enquiry on his face, at the policeman, but he was obviously not prepared to say anything further until they were alone, out of earshot of the other policemen. They walked for a while down to the water's edge. There was a consignment of bales and Steve automatically produced a knife and cut the corner of one of them—wool, then:

"What did you mean bad news." He held up the knife as he spoke: "I want to warn you that I am a bad loser."

Farjas shrugged:

"It is not fair. I will not know for sure until I check in with headquarters at eight."

Steve began to move away and Farjas said:

"There is a cafe by the dock entrance. Take some coffee for your headache. I will join you when I have finished here—promise."

Steve nodded and turned away to walk the way they had come. Farjas was obviously a bundle of nerves but he was convinced that the policeman would tell him all he knew, given time, not pushed. He made straight for the cafe and settled himself with a cup of coffee and a newspaper to wait for the policeman to reappear.

On the alert for further trouble, Johnny slept in a chair in his room, still dressed. After the killing of Henri, he had returned to the hotel by a circuitous route, with the added felicity of depositing the stolen car back on the same spot from which he had taken it. He had then returned to the hotel and had been almost disappointed to find that the two seedy billiard players had given up their long, pointless game.

The bed had not looked particularly inviting and Johnny, who was fussy in such details (a reaction to the privations he had suffered as a mercenary in the Congo) had thought it best not to chance it anyway.

He woke early, the rising sun playing on his face. Though stiff from the cramping shape of the chair, he was otherwise rested and alert—and well aware that today was the day. But first he had to call Steve.

He found the Paris number, then went downstairs to obtain the necessary jeton from the old woman on the desk. She had been in situ when he had finally returned the night before, and he was beginning to suspect that she was permanently chained to her post. At least it would explain her aura of evil temper. He thanked her for the jeton, went over to the wall phone, dialled the Paris number and waited impatiently for the phone to be answered the other end.

The number that Steve had given him was to a private line in his office and it was Sally who picked up the receiver:

"Hello, U.S. Embassy. Mr. Ventura's office."

Deray breathed a sigh of relief:

"Is Mr. Ventura there please?"

There was a pause, then:

"No, I'm afraid he's out of town at the moment."

"Where?"

"I'm not at liberty to divulge his whereabouts."

Johnny swallowed the rude words that would have come so easily:

"May I leave an urgent message then. Will you be contacting him?"

"Certainly, Sir. He ordered me to be in touch if it warranted his attention on his present business."

"Right. Will you find him please and ask him to call room Number Ten at 432721 Marseilles. Will you just tell him that it has to do with the Contract."

"But, Sir, your name."

"I can't give it to you, anyway he doesn't need it. Just tell him it's to do with the Contract. He'll know what I mean."

"Oh, Steve—I mean Mr. Ventura is always being so secretive. Okay, he's to call Room Ten at Marseilles 432721."

"Yes, that's right. Thanks very much. Goodbye." He slammed down the receiver and turned to remount the stairs. As he reached the angle at the top of the first flight he saw out of the corner of his eye the narrow swing door of the hotel entrance open and Kurt come cautiously inside. He was out of sight before Brizard's man had a chance to glance up and spot him. He had no illusions. The old crone would give out his room number and the thug would be up for him in a few minutes.

He entered his room and shut the door quietly behind him in case Kurt was already on the stairs and would be alerted by any sudden movement. From the bed he snatched a pillow, then, holding it in one hand and his gun in the other, he opened the door to the small washroom that stood to the left of the door to the room, and stood by the wall on the other side of the hallway door.

He didn't have long to wait. After a moment there came the sound of one set of cautious footsteps moving slowly down the corridor towards his room. They halted, there was a pause, then a knock on the door. Johnny pitched his voice at a level which he hoped would make it sound as if he was on the far side of the room:

"Who is it?"

Kurt's voice was muffled through the woodwork:

"Police."

A pause then Johnny called:

"Come in."

The handle turned and the door swung open, masking Johnny from sight. Through the crack, he saw Kurt move forward, one hand still on the door handle, the other holding a lethal-looking snub-nosed automatic. Johnny let him take two paces into the room, then stepped forward, pushed the pillow at Kurt's face so that the man tried to weave and dodge rather than aim with his own gun. Johnny brought his gun up against the pillow and fired. Only one shot was necessary and, with a push, Johnny made the dying man fall into the tiny washroom, the basin supporting his falling body. The only noise from him came from his gun as it fell with a clatter on the porcelain of the basin.

During the next few minutes, Johnny worked with lightning speed. He dragged the body over to the wardrobe, keeping the pillow against the man's head to keep the spread of blood to a minimum. Still holding the man up, he opened the wardrobe door, then lifted him inside, propping him up so that he would stay upright when the wardrobe door was closed. With any luck it would be the hotel's next guest who would find this gruesome room-mate. Johnny had no intention of staying at the Hotel Miami for a moment longer than was necessary.

He shut the door of the wardrobe and looked at his handiwork. It was sagging but he felt it would hold up. He slipped Kurt's automatic into his own pocket, then settled down to wait for Steve's call.

At the same time that the new drama of murder was being played out in Johnny's seedy hotel room, not a quarter of a mile away, in the cafe at the side of the docks, Farjas had rejoined Steve Ventura. The latter ordered him a cup of coffee and asked:

"Any more news?"

Farjas looked depressed and ran a hand over his pale features. In contrast to his earlier look, he now seemed tired and listless, a pallor creeping over his tan:

"Only bad. I checked with headquarters."

"Well?"

Farjas managed a weak smile:

"One of the orders was that I was not to tell you this."

Steve looked the man straight in the eye:

"And you will obey that order?"

Farjas chuckled:

"What do you think." Then his face was grim again as he went on: "Jacques Brizard is no longer under surveillance, nor is anyone who is connected with him in the City."

Steve was shocked and made no attempt to disguise it. This was the last thing he had expected:

"Why?"

Farjas gave a Gallic shrug of all-embracing proportions, a gesture that encompassed everything and nothing:

"Brizard is giving a huge Charity Ball tonight. He cannot be collecting any drugs. It must be that they are not coming in tonight."

Ventura shook his head as if unable to believe his ears:

"Do you really believe that."

Again the shrug:

"It doesn't matter what I believe. I have been told to leave him entirely alone. Those are my orders."

"Whose orders?"

"Departmental orders. Marsac seemed as unhappy as I am. I think it is higher up than us—perhaps even the politicians in Paris."

"Forget the orders," urged Steve. "Farjas, help me to get him."

Farjas shook his head:

"I've got a family. I can't change the world."

"Maybe you should try just this once." Steve could feel the anger welling up in him. He liked this man well enough, but he had liked Frank Matthews too. Frank had been a man with a wife and family, Frank had made his pathetic attempt to change the world and had died for it. Who did this Frenchman think he was. Steve wanted to explain to him, to exhort him, but realised, even as he thought it, that it would produce no good result. Farjas said:

"Well, I have to go—oh, there is one more thing. After the killing at the yacht club last night, Brizard and his mistress did not return to the villa, but went aboard Brizard's yacht. They were joined by his daughter, Lucienne first thing this morning."

"Why?"

"Presumably to be close at hand for the arrangements for the Charity Ball tonight. The yacht is anchored near the club."

Steve nodded and thanked the man before he paid for the coffees, then got down from his stool:

"I will go back to the hotel."

"And then?"

Steve shrugged:

"I have no family. Perhaps I will try to change the world."

Steve walked back to the hotel and went straight to his room. He had not been in the room for more than five minutes when the phone rang:

"Hello, Steve? This is Sally."

He sighed:

"Hi. What do you want?"

"Well, it's always nice to be appreciated. Nothing important, really. I had a call and—."

"Who from."

"That's just the thing. He wouldn't leave his name, just said that it was about the Contract and you would understand."

Steve sat bolt upright:

"What was the rest of the message, quick." As he spoke, he groped in his pocket for a pen and, as Sally gave him the number, he scribbled it down on the scratchpad by the phone that the hotel thoughtfully provided. When she had finished the message, he checked the number back to her and there was a new liveliness and excitement in his voice:

"Thanks, Sally. Anything else."

"Well, Fred Williams is still after you about the budget. I haven't told him where you are—just that you're out of town with a hot lead for a few days. Chief—."

"Yes."

"Be careful."

"Thanks." He breathed this last word down the phone, before depressing the bar and cutting off the call. The switchboard came back on after a moment's impatient wait and Steve gave the number he had been given by Sally.

He seemed to wait forever before a shaky female voice answered the phone and asked him what was his pleasure. He could imagine that he was talking to a seedy waterfront hotel or boarding house, the sort that would only have a pay phone for outgoing calls, though incoming one's would then be taken, put through to the rooms and charged for on the bill. He said:

"Room ten, please."

A moment later Johnny's voice came on the line:

"Yes."

Ventura spoke quickly:

"Don't talk. Come to the Hotel Massena, Room 112, as soon as you can."

In spite of Steve's instruction, Johnny said:

"I can't make it in daylight. I'll come as soon as it's dark."

"Why not?"

"Your fault mainly. The police are after me."

"Sorry, Johnny." A moment later he heard a tremendous crash over the phone and asked urgently

"What happened."

Johnny took a minute to survey the damage done to the wardrobe before he answered. The door had slipped open under the weight of Kurt's dead body and the latter had crashed down onto the floor. At last he said with a trace of humour:

"Somebody just dropped in. I'll come over as soon as I've tidied him up."

"Okay." He hung up. The laugh in Johnny's voice had told him that he at least was still enthusiastic about his job. He also knew now that he would not carry out the Contract before he had met with him, so there was still a chance for them both to nail Brizard legally.

He settled down to wait impatiently for his old friend's arrival, occupying the time by thinking out ways of protecting him from the results of the fight with the police at Mulhouse. There was no easy way that he could see—but at least Marsac had been willing to admit that the police had no direct evidence yet that Johnny was involved, either in the north, or in the killing at the yacht club. It didn't matter what they might speculate. As long as Steve stuck to his identification of the body of Minieri in the Marseilles morgue as that of Johnny, there would be nothing the authorities could do, provided he got to Johnny first.

CHAPTER FOURTEEN

The lobby of the Massena Hotel was a bustle of noise and light when Johnny Deray, dressed in the suit he had bought off the peg and the heavy overcoat, came up the steps and passed into the hotel.

The establishment was totally geared to the huge charity dinner and ball that was just getting underway. Johnny moved rapidly through the lobby to the stairs. As he reached the bottom of them, a door opened from the ladies cloakroom and Madame Apcar issued forth, dressed to kill. She saw Johnny, clapped her hands with delight and grabbed his arm:

"No, no, the gala is this way."

Johnny tried to break away from her with gentle politeness:

"I'm sorry. I have to go upstairs to see somebody. It is a business matter, urgent."

She hung on grimly, looking up at him, her false eyelashes going at nineteen to the dozen:

"Later, come with me."

Johnny allowed himself to be propelled across the lobby to the entrance to the buffet:

"But I'm not dressed properly for the occasion."

"It doesn't matter." At the entrance to the room, Madame Apcar paused to take a flower emblem from a seller who stood submissively not demanding payment, which she then placed in Johnny's button hole:

"There you are now properly dressed."

"Thank you."

They went on inside. At a table just inside the door, Jacques Brizard had seated his party so that he would be able to see anyone who arrived and choose to greet them or let them pass, depending on their importance, either to him or the charity—it would also allow him to slip out easily without being noticed when the time came for his rendezvous. Lucienne was sitting on his right, looking pale and out of sorts, having obviously missed Johnny and been offended by his broken promise of the night before. The Countess was also for the moment seated with them.

Madame Apcar dragged him to the table:

"Look who I've found."

Brizard and the others looked up. For a moment, Brizard's eyes blazed hatred, then were masked again. Lucienne showed only hurt. As the level of tension rose so that even Madame Apcar herself began to think that she had done the wrong thing, the Countess, oblivious to the relationships between the others present smiled a welcome:

"Ah, the population specialist. Are you still killing people?"

Under other circumstances the question would have been funny. In the silence that followed, Brizard leant over, whispered something to Lucienne, then got up and left the room. Johnny watched him go, then:

"Whenever I can."

Lucienne rose from her place, came over and kissed him lightly on the cheek:

"Where were you."

He responded to the kiss:

"Something came up. I couldn't call you." All the time, his mind was racing. Brizard had probably gone to alert Calmet and his men. Any moment now someone might walk into the room and kill him:

"Where did your father go?"

"He went to make a phone call."

Johnny was visibly relieved. At least that meant he had a few minutes to get out of the room and up to Steve. Outwardly, he appeared calm and asked:

"Will he be long."

Lucienne managed a thin smile, insulted that Johnny should be more interested in her father's absence than in her own presence:

"Who knows? One time he was gone for two weeks. Why don't you relax and join us?"

He gently took her hand off his arm:

"No, I have to see someone first." He turned away, then seemed to feel guilt at the abruptness of his departure and said over his shoulder: "I'll be back. I shouldn't be too long."

"When?"

He came back, took her chin between his thumb and forefinger, then kissed her coolly on the lips. As she responded to him, he backed a pace and said:

"I'll be back."

As he left the room and recrossed the lobby, Lucienne sat down, and Madame Apcar put a consoling hand on her shoulder when she saw that the younger girl was close to tears.

Brizard was in a phone box near the desk, his back to Johnny as he crossed to the stairs. He did not see him and seemed to be talking at some length to a patient listener on the other end of the phone. Johnny went quickly up the stairs to Steve's room. Steve had left the key in his door and Johnny turned it and went quickly inside without knocking, his other hand on the butt of his gun in his coat pocket.

Steve was lying on the bed in his shirt sleeves and swung to an upright position as Johnny slammed the door behind him and threw the key down on the bed:

"I would never leave my key in the door. You've got clumsy in your old age, Steve."

Steve snapped without preamble:

"Forget about the damned key. Are you pushing drugs for Jacques Brizard and his people?"

Johnny frowned, taken aback by the question and the vehemence of the questioner:

"What are you smoking," he managed at last.

Steve was silent for a moment. When he spoke again, his voice was quieter, more controlled:

"Look, please level with me. What about the junk you had at the bunker in Mulhouse."

Deray nodded, suddenly understanding:

"Look, Steve, you should know me better than that. Brizard set me up. I'm clean. You know damned well I'd never push drugs—and incidentally, I don't rob banks that often, either."

"No, you only kill people."

It was Johnny's turn to be angry:

"Now, wait a minute, don't evade the issue. Okay, so I kill people, that's my job. What was all that bank robbery thing about."

Steve nodded:

"I'm sorry about that. There was a chance to nail Brizard legally, so I did the only thing I could think to to get you stopped for long enough to cancel the Contract."

"Jeez, Steve. You must be mad. You'll never stop that bugger, except with a bullet, anyway, that's why I came to see you. I can set Brizard up for a kill tonight."

Steve strode over to the dressing table, opened a drawer, produced a gun and put it into his pants pocket:

"Forget it. I've changed my mind. I'm sorry, Johnny, but I just don't need you on this job any more."

He walked over to the window and stood, staring out into the darkness over the port. Johnny followed him, very angry:

"Oh yes, cancel the Contract. Well, you won't get your bloody money back, that's for sure."

"Shove the money—but I'm going to take Brizard myself."

Johnny sat down heavily on the edge of the bed and began to laugh. Steve whirled round from the window:

"What's so funny?"

"You. . . . You're going to kill Brizard."

"If I have to—why? You think I can't?"

Johnny fought back his laughter:

"No, Steve, sorry, I don't think it's on, but if it was, I'm sure you could do it. But you could use some help. Everybody needs a little help once in a while."

Steve saw his point:

"You have any ideas?"

"It's not my style to accept payment for work I don't then do. It's a matter of professional pride. Besides, what are friends for if they can't give a little help."

Their eyes met and suddenly they were both laughing. The tension between them drained away and it was a moment before either of them was recovered enough to speak. Then Steve said:

"Do you know that guy Brizard's downstairs right now enjoying himself at a party."

Johnny was overtaken by a new paroxym of laughter:

"Oh, boy, can you use some help, Steve. You've really lost your touch completely."

"What do you mean?"

"He's not downstairs."

"Of course he is."

"No. He's taking delivery of a consignment of drugs —the largest he's ever handled."

Steve shook his head:

"No, that's off for tonight because of the party."

"No, Steve. That's precisely why it's on, what better cover would he have but the charity do."

Steve pouted:

"Well, if you're so Goddamn clever, where is he?"

Johnny savoured the moment. He glanced at his watch:

"Right about now he's meeting his chief contact at a place called the Buenos Aires. I've looked it up, it's on the Rue de la Charite. If we hurry, we'll catch him there."

Steve put on his jacket, his face split by a smile:

"You always used to be right. Let's go."

Johnny held up a hand, advocating caution:

"Is there a back way out?"

"Why?"

"Well, he saw me arrive just before he left. If I know anything about him, the hall and the stairs are probably being covered by his goons, just waiting for me to re-appear."

Steve nodded:

"Follow me."

They left Steve's room after a cautious glance down the corridor, which proved empty, then made for the service stairs. This led down to the kitchens and a quick glance showed nobody except normal-looking kitchen staff and waiters hurrying through from the ballroom with special food and drink orders. They walked quickly through the kitchens to the back entrance of the hotel, its over-riding squalor a sharp contrast with the baroque splendour of the front of the building.

Steve went cautiously ahead, then turned back:

"All clear."

"They went down the alley that came out to the main road a block away from the hotel." Johnny said:

"We can walk it quite quickly from here. It's near the centre of the old town."

Steve was puzzled:

"How can he accept the dope there, how can it be brought in?"

Johnny shrugged as they walked:

"Well, it's clever. It's the last place anyone would expect a big drug handover to be arranged, so doubtless he's sorted out the difficulties. As the man said, "Let's hold our water till we get there."

The Rue de la Charite was a comparatively short and bleak road in the old town. For almost one side—the side on which the Buenos Aires Cafe was located, a huge wall backed the pavement, the wall that blocked off the old Hospice de la Charite, one of the oldest of the architectural treasures of Marseilles, now alas, in decay and totally blocked from view, except for its main gates which were round the corner of the block.

Johnny and Steve came cautiously down the street from the opposite end of the wall to the main gates and the cafe and, when they drew level with the cafe in the shadows, they leant forward and peered into the lit window. The bar-cafe was nearly empty. A girl was serving a drink to one man at the bar, three children were playing on a pinball machine but, at the back, Steve spotted a man on the phone, a man he recognised as Fortuit, Brizard's driver. Johnny pointed by way of confirmation:

"He works for Brizard."

A moment later, Fortuit finished his call, hung up the receiver and turned to leave the bar. The two watchers shrank back into the shadow of the wall. As he came out of the cafe, Fortuit turned in the opposite direction from the two men, then stopped where it was possible to see a gap in the wall, leant against the side of the gap and lit up a cigarette. He was obviously on look-out for some reason—and this was confirmed a moment later as Steve's question as to how the handover was to take place was answered.

There came the low hum of a machine and, suddenly, above them was a helicopter, large crates strapped to its sides. It moved slowly above the buildings, hovered for a moment over the Hospice, then, finding its landing spot, it sank down beyond the wall. A moment later the engine cut out and the silence of the street returned.

Johnny and Steve glanced at one another, then at Fortuit, standing by the gap in the wall. They both nodded and began to creep forward. There was no need to speak, they both knew that Fortuit would have to be eliminated for them to get inside the Hospice and take Brizard in the act.

Johnny signalled that he would walk along the street, leaving Steve to take the man. A moment later, he staggered into the centre of the road as if he had just come out of the cafe. He realised it would take Fortuit a minute or two to realise that he had not seen him inside and a minute or two was all he hoped Steve needed, or he would be a dead man.

He began to stagger drunkenly down the road, waving happily at the guard, whose eyes were fixed nervously on him. It was too dark for him to be recognised yet, but as he staggered closer, he knew he would be in great danger.

Steve had got past the lighted windows of the cafe without being spotted and was now moving forward in the shadow of the wall, only a few yards from Fortuit. The man let the cigarette dangle down in surprise as he recognised Johnny Deray. His hand went to the gun in his pocket and, as he drew it, Steve sprang, taking Fortuit by the throat.

Fortuit's neck broke like a dry stick and Steve let the body fall as Johnny joined him. He grinned:

"You haven't lost your touch, Steve."

The American shot him a baleful glance, then stepped over the body and slipped through the hole in the wall. Johnny quickly followed and they found themselves immersed in the darkened cloisters of the old Hospice. They could see light at the end of the cloisters, so the main activity would be taking place round the helicopter which must have landed on the open space in the centre of the Hospice. The two men moved slowly forward in the darkness, drawing their guns as they went. In the distance, they could hear shouted orders from Brizard and indistinguishable voices speaking in reply.

They were close to the end of their cover when they were able to see Brizard, who was himself supervising the unloading of the packages of drugs from the helicopter to a van. His own car was parked at the far side, close to the open gates of the main entrance, and turned ready for a quick getaway of it proved necessary.

Calmet and the pilot were involved in the actual unloading. Another man stood in the shadows next to Brizard. Johnny, whose ears were more tuned to danger, heard a noise above them and signalled to Steve that there was at least one other man—a guard—overhead.

Steve nodded his thanks and they watched as they were figuring out what to do next. It was at that moment that Brizard turned to the man in the shadows. They were too far away to catch the words, but, a moment later, the man moved forward into the light and Steve let out an involuntary gasp, for the man with Jacques Brizard, his partner in the deal, was Inspector Briac of the Surete.

CHAPTER FIFTEEN

As Steve Ventura and Johnny Deray crouched in the shadow of the cloisters watching the activity in the central courtyard, Wilson stood on the level above them, machine gun in hand. He was as unaware of their presence at that moment as they were of his, but he too was overlooking the work going on below him, hidden from the sight of those who were working. Jacques Brizard and his lieutenant knew he was there; Briac and the helicopter pilot were unsuspecting.

Brizard turned to Briac, his face beaming:

"Well, my friend. A very successful operation, don't you think." He paused to glance at his watch. Then: "I will leave Calmet to finish up here and take everything away. It's almost all in the van anyway. I have to get back to the ball—some of my guests may have noticed that I am missing by now."

Briac smiled as he stepped alongside Brizard towards the car:

"Thank you for the wine. I even gave a bottle to Steve Ventura. It amused me to think that he would be drinking a gift from you."

Brizard frowned and grunted:

"That was taking an unnecessary risk, wasn't it. He might have checked up who had bought the consignment."

Briac shrugged:

"These Americans. They want so much to be loved, they will trust almost anybody. They never look at the details that are laid out right under their noses. They will always take the complicated route to an answer."

Brizard, his hand on the handle of the door of his Rolls, turned abruptly:

"They are not the only ones. It is a great pity to me that you did not find out about the Contract that Ventura took out with Johnny Deray until he had wormed his way into my confidence."

Briac was still unconcerned by the criticism:

"But I knew of it all along." There was a new note in his voice which had not been there before and the obsequiousness that had been present before slipped away from him. Brizard glanced down and saw that the policeman had a gun in his hand:

"Don't be so impatient, my friend. I don't think you have to get back to your party at all."

Brizard's eyes were bulging with disbelief. He turned towards Calmet, only to see that the helicopter pilot had followed Briac's cue and also had a gun drawn, covering the other man, who had his hands in the air.

Both Brizard and Calmet looked in every direction other than the place where they knew Wilson was waiting and watching, but Brizard prayed for him to make his move quickly. After a moment, Brizard spoke, his voice still calm:

"What on earth is going on here, please, Briac. Are you putting me under arrest, or something?"

Briac's smile was broad as he shook his head:

"Nothing as simple as that, Brizard. I am now going to kill you—you and Calmet."

Brizárd's mouth was a grim line as he understood:

"So then you will be left with the shipment."

"You have it in one. It is so simple. I am not even in Marseilles at all. Steve Ventura will think that Deray could not be stopped and has killed you—the case will be closed almost before it is investigated."

Brizard nodded and passed a weary hand over his forehead. This was the emergency signal to Wilson and he prayed that the man was in a position to obey the instruction. An instant later, his prayer was answered. There was a noise from above and Wilson appeared, standing on a parapet above the cloisters. He raised the machine gun and fired a short burst—short but effective as Briac screamed, the gun dropping from his hand as he clutched his stomach where he had been hit. He staggered away from Brizard, diving behind a pile of rubble that shielded him from any further bullets.

Wilson ducked back as the pilot turned his gun towards this new distraction. Calmet immediately launched himself at the man. Caught off-balance, his gun went one way, the man the other. Calmet snatched out his own gun and shot the pilot between the eyes in one fluid movement, that took Johnny's breath away with its professional expertise as he and Steve watched in amazement from their hiding place.

As for Brizard, he had turned, opened the door and had climbed into the Rolls-Royce. He started up as Calmet ran to join him and it was at that moment that Johnny took a hand. He aimed and fired, cutting Calmet down in mid-stride. The man was dead before he hit the ground.

Johnny leant over to Steve:

"I'm going after Brizard, round this side. I'll see you

later." Before Steve had time to reply to acknowledge him, he had disappeared into the darkness and was dodging back up the cloisters, towards the far side working round to the main entrance.

For the moment, it seemed to Steve that he was helplessly pinned down as Brizard slowly turned the huge car, preparatory to driving away from the scene, unhurt and clean. Above him, he knew there crouched a man with a machine gun. Until he knew just where, he could not move. But he could stand the inactivity no longer and decided to take a chance. He dashed forward to the Rolls-Royce, gun in hand, just as Johnny emerged from cover on the far side of the central courtyard. The Rolls-Royce shot forward and disappeared through the main archway before he had a chance to get off a shot.

Steve turned quickly to try to regain safe cover. Wilson was standing in the open above him, aiming the gun at Steve. Johnny spotted him and started running towards Steve:

"Get back. Look out."

Steve dived for the nearest cover immediately as Wilson tried to pick him up in the barrel of the gun. He turned instead to Johnny, firing a short burst. Johnny came forward a few more paces, his gun coming up, then collapsed, falling on his face in the dirt.

In the moment he had given him, Steve had ducked down the cloisters to the far end. Now he emerged from cover, his gun ready to fire before Wilson could turn to dive for cover or defend himself. The gunman crashed to his death in the dust a few yards away from the dying Johnny.

Ignoring any danger that might still come from the one other man still alive in the Hospice, Inspector Briac, Steve put his gun in his pocket and ran to Johnny Deray, kneeling by his side. He said quietly:

"Well, you did it again. Only this time there doesn't seem to be much I can do in return."

Johnny's eyes flickered open and, with a herculean effort, he managed to give a lopsided smile:

"Like I said, Steve. We can all use a little help."

His eyes clouded over and the rattle came from his throat as he choked on his own blood. Steve felt the tears hot and stinging in his eyes as he watched the life ebb out of his friend. He knelt for a little while beside him in lonely remembrance.

It was only as he stood up that he remembered Briac and moved towards the rubble where the man had hidden with greater caution. The job was far from finished now, even though the delivery of the drugs had been thwarted. The abandoned van and helicopter lights still lit the central area and Steve had no trouble in picking his way through to where Briac was located, his gun ready, his nerves straining for a sign of a counter-attack.

But the moment he rounded the rubble, he saw that Inspector Briac was in no condition to fight back, was finished. He was clutching his stomach, the blood seeping between his fingers as he coughed and groaned the remaining minutes of his life away.

Steve put the gun away again and squatted down by him:

"It's over, Briac. You were playing both sides, then?"

Briac managed his smile through pain and blood, for just one last time:

"Nothing personal, just business. If Deray had been quicker and killed Brizard, then I'd have had everything. . . ."

"And then what?"

Briac's voice was faint but still defiant:

"Somewhere in the South Seas—a quiet life."

Steve shook his head sadly:

"There is no such thing for men like you. Your greed would have driven you on. The taste of corruption leads to more corruption. And to think I trusted you."

He stopped speaking. There was no point in going on. Briac's eyes stared at him sightlessly. He was the only survivor, the only one left alive—until he remembered Jacques Brizard.

For a long time, Steve Ventura stayed at the Hospice de la Charite, sitting amid the carnage around him. There was something he must do for Johnny Deray and it would take a little thinking out to tell him what was the best decision. His training as a policeman told him that he must call Farjas, bring him to the place and explain what had happened. With his evidence as an eye-witness, Brizard would at least be arrested and brought to trial. But something in Steve told him that this was not enough. Brizard was too clever to be caught like this. If only the eye-witness account of one man stood between him and liberty, there were no lengths to which he would not go to eliminate the possibility. No, the only thing he could do was eliminate the cancer, kill Jacques Brizard—carry out the Contract that he had given his friend, that had cost Johnny Deray his life. He whispered:

"For you, Johnny, for you."

Then he turned on his heel and walked out through the main gates of the Hospice.

In the street outside, he made his way to the Cafe Buenos Aires. He entered, walked straight to the phone, dialled police headquarters and asked for Farjas. As soon as the policeman was on the line, he said:

"Get this and get this fast. The drugs are at the Hospice de la Charite now."

He slammed down the phone before Farjas could speak, turned and walked out of the cafe and along the darkened street. As he turned the first corner on his way back to the hotel and Brizard, he could hear the sounds of police sirens in the distance. Farjas had wasted no time.

Jacques Brizard let the Rolls-Royce slip into its reserved parking place outside the hotel. He sat in the car for a moment, looking at himself in the driving mirror, making sure that the events that had just occurred had left no mark on him.

When he was satisfied, he got out of the car and went quickly up the hotel steps. He still felt a little shaky, but this passed off with each pace he took. He checked his topcoat in the cloakroom then went to wash his hands before emerging re-entering the ballroom looking as smart as when he had left. From the moment he entered the ballroom, he was exuding urbane charm as if the events of the past hour had not occurred. Madame Apcar was dancing with a svelte young man, but Lucienne was still sitting at their table, glancing miserably towards the entrance, waiting for Johnny to reappear as he had promised.

She brightened a little as she saw her father who moved swiftly to her side and said with an urgency that surprised her and belied his appearance:

"Let's dance."

As she stood up he took her arm and led her quickly onto the floor. She hung back and asked:

"Father, what's the matter."

"Wait until we're on the floor." She obeyed him and he held her close as they went into the dance. She could feel his body trembling close to her as if he were very afraid and she pressed herself all the closer. Madame Apcar, suddenly noticing him, pushed away her partner, aware that Jacques would be angry with her if he saw her flirting with a young man. But he went past, his daughter in his arms, not noticing or caring. She stomped back to the table by the door and sat down with an angry frown.

Lucienne and her father were still dancing in silence when Steve Ventura climbed the steps to the hotel, walking like a man in a trance, crossed the lobby and stood at the entrance to the ballroom. The noise of the company seemed to wake him and he looked round until he had spotted Brizard. He saw at once that he would not be able to reach the man through the crowd without causing a disturbance which would destroy his plan. It was Brizard's mistress who provided the key to his dilemma.

She looked up admiringly at the newcomer, noticing his bearing and, with a glance to see that Brizard was not in sight, she rose and walked over to him, her eyelashes fluttering:

"Are you against pollution?"

"What?"

"I said, are you against pollution?" A little frown appeared on her smooth brow. This didn't seem to be her night and she made a mental note to change her hairstyle. She seemed to be losing her allure.

Steve dragged his eyes off Brizard and glanced down at the woman who had addressed him. He recognised Brizard's mistress from the picture in his file at once. Her words finally seeped through the single-mindedness of his brain and he managed a smile:

"Yes, of course, that is why I am here."

"Good, then you will need a flower."

She took one from a nearby table arrangement and reached up on tiptoe to place it in his lapel. He held her arm to steady her and it seemed almost an accident when she fell forward, pressing herself against him. As a plan half-formed in his mind: he heard himself ask:

"Shall we dance."

She answered eagerly and almost dragged him on to the floor. He could see Lucienne and her father on the far side of the throng. To anyone who did not know that they were father and daughter they would be taken for lovers. Steve began to manoeuvre through the other dancers, pushing Madame Apcar before him, determined to reach his enemy before the dancing stopped.

On the far side of the floor, Brizard had not yet noticed Steve Ventura's arrival. Lucienne had waited patiently while they danced in silence, now she smiled as he cleared his throat and said quietly:

"I've had an idea."

"Well?"

"I think that tomorrow, when this is all over, we should up anchor and go for a nice long cruise somewhere."

Lucienne laughed:

"That sounds lovely, but where?"

Brizard sighed and held her closer:

"Some warm, safe place."

They turned in time to the music and he stiffened as he spotted Steve and his mistress dancing towards him. Lucienne glanced in the same direction:

"What's the matter?"

"Nothing," he replied, turning her so that she faced another direction. A few moments later, the couples were close and, as Brizard was forced to look into Steve Ventura's eyes, he saw hatred and death and felt a mortal fear.

Steve whirled Madame Apcar round so that he could keep his eyes constantly on his quarry as the other man tried to dance away through the crowd. Soon he was immediately behind Brizard and he surreptitiously slipped his gun out of his pocket, hiding it behind Madame Apcar's long hair as his arms encircled her. As he got close to Brizard, he placed the barrel of the gun at the base of the man's spine, then pulled the trigger.

The closeness muffled the sound of the shot. For a moment it seemed that Brizard would stagger and fall, but he leaned over his daughter and she kept him upright, assuming he had slipped on the floor. She had noticed nothing.

Steve slipped the gun back into his pocket, his task completed, then whirled Madame Apcar back across the floor, further and further away from his victim. As he faced Brizard for one last time, he nodded at the dying man, who automatically nodded back, an acknowledgement that he had lost and the other man had won.

As soon as Steve had reached the edge of the dance floor nearest the entrance, he let go of Madame Apcar, swept her a low bow and then walked out before she had a chance to react. She was left dazed by the speed of her encounter and sudden abandonment.

On the dance floor Lucienne became suddenly alarmed by the growing sluggish weight of her father. She looked at his face and was alarmed to see a greyness on it. She snapped:

"Who was that man?"

Brizard managed one last tight smile:

"The man who killed me."

It was as if these words released him. He swayed away from his daughter, then crashed to the floor. Lucienne knelt down beside him and shook his arm, but one glance at his face told her that he was dead. She began to scream uncontrollably.

Steve was at the entrance to the hotel as he heard

her screams rip out through the air. He knew now that the job was finished.

He walked slowly away from the Hotel Massena, down the street towards the docks. He was totting up the balance sheet that had ended with the pay-off of the death of Jacques Brizard, the elimination of one major link in the chain of international drug trafficking.

Frank Matthews and Marcus had died so that Brizard would survive. Now Johnny Deray and Inspector Briac had died so that the beast might die. The result was that thousands of the innocent would live.

Steve Ventura held his head up and breathed in the fresh night air. He had made the right decision. The Marseilles Contract had been fulfilled.

THE END

STILL ON THE BESTSELLER LISTS AFTER A YEAR!

THE DAY OF THE JACKAL by FREDERICK FORSYTH

One man with a rifle who can change the course of history.
Who is he?
Can he be found before *The Day of the Jackal?*

'As a political thriller it is virtually in a class by itself; subtle, fast-moving, superbly written, unputdownable, easily beating Ian Fleming on his own ground. The entire French background is beautifully atmospheric —down to the last whiff of Gauloise.'
—*Sunday Times*

'A compelling, utterly enthralling first novel . . . some of the tensest thriller writing I can remember reading.' —*Sunday Express*

'The tension, excitement and pace are brilliantly maintained to the last page.' —*Sunday Mirror*

THE DAY OF THE JACKAL

works beautifully . . . I was held spellbound . . . riveted to this chilling, superbly researched story. A remarkable ring of authority . . . a superb piece of mystery.' —*Guardian*

'Electrifyingly exciting . . . within or without the pages of fiction there can rarely have been such a meticulously efficient, cold-blooded human killer. Mr. Forsyth is clever, very clever and immensely entertaining.' —*Daily Telegraph*